JB SCHROEDER

second chance love affair

Love That Lasts

BOOK 2

Two Feet
Press

11923 NE Sumner St., Ste 843916
Portland, Oregon 97220

Print Edition 1.0
ISBN-13: 978-1-943561-20-9

To James

———

My Husband
My Rock

A white Lincoln Town Car pulled up, but as far as Darcy Hellston was concerned, her ride home from Glenmead College may as well have been a hearse. It was, after all, abruptly, remorselessly, carrying her away from this life.

Her eyes filled and her lip wobbled—until she bit down hard to stop it and fisted her hands.

The driver stepped out and came around the car, but her father, Randolph Hellston, didn't wait for anyone. As he unfolded his tall frame from the back, she saw him set a portfolio of paperwork on the seat. Of course he'd worked on the way up. Surely, he'd work on the way back, too. If she was lucky, she wouldn't have to say more than five words.

He followed the walkway to where she stood, just outside of the apartment building that had been her home all of sophomore year. His face was as regal and stern as ever, and his expression didn't soften as he kissed her on the cheek. Her father was not a hugger. Just as well. A hug would have turned her into a puddle.

His eyes swept the area around her, and his nostrils flared. "Please tell me you are packed. I've got a meeting I've got to get back for."

She had tucked her duffel, suitcases, and hamper stuffed full of bedding behind a bush. Because it was near a stairwell exit, she had hoped it didn't appear too suspicious. She led the way and grabbed as many items as she could manage.

"Please, miss," the driver said. "I'll get them."

She tried to smile at him, to let him know it was okay. She needed this done fast. Before any of her roommates, especially Jeremy, returned from their finals.

One thought of Jeremy, and the tears spilled over. *Damn*. Darcy bent her head as she shoved bags into the trunk and surreptitiously swiped her cheeks. She'd done loads of crying already. She needed to keep it together now.

As the driver added the remainder of her things to the trunk, her father opened the back door for her. "There's no one you need to tell you are going?"

She was sure he meant the landlord, the bursar, someone official. But all she could think of was Jeremy. She hadn't said goodbye. She couldn't. She hadn't known in advance that her dad would be arriving this early. Jeremy would try to reach her, she knew. But she'd have to avoid his calls. Because the minute she heard his voice, she'd break down. She'd tell him everything—things she didn't want him to know. And Jeremy being Jeremy, he'd want to help. But he couldn't. No one could.

She sucked in a shaky breath. "No," she told her father, and ducked into the car.

Her father slid into the other side, and they pulled away. Darcy squeezed her eyes shut and turned her face toward the window. She didn't want Jeremy wasting his time on her. He was the handsómest, sexiest boy she'd ever met, yet he wasn't cocky or obnoxious or immature like most of the boys she knew. He was real, down to earth, and fun—but also serious, smart, and hardworking. He would go places. She knew it.

God, she would give anything to go with him. But she was a losing prospect no matter how you cut it. She wasn't good enough for him, and she never would be. And she refused to be someone who would hold him back. But she'd always love him. Always.

Suddenly her hands—which she hadn't realized were clenched together on her lap—were covered by one of her father's. Her eyes popped open. She saw real concern on his face. It was untoward for a Hellston to display emotion in public. She supposed sitting in a car with a driver and her father was public enough for him.

"You know you don't have to worry about anything, right?"

He had no idea, she thought, but she nodded. What else could she do?

"I'll always take care of my little girl." He patted her hand, adjusted his readers, and settled back into his work.

She unclenched her fists and wiped her palms on her jeans.

Maybe she was never meant to be anything more than her parents' daughter—a rich, pampered socialite.

No matter that she'd tried to make the most of this

opportunity to start over in college. No matter how hard she'd worked, how determined she'd been, how deeply she wanted it. She'd tried even harder after she'd met Jeremy. God, she'd tried so damn hard.

Yet it hadn't mattered. Not one bit. Shame flooded her and roasted her cheeks. Maybe she should have just been the live-life-to-the-fullest party girl she'd pretended to be, instead of sneaking off in secret to work, getting up early, putting her whole heart into it. At least then it would have been easier to give it all up and live in her family's world.

But no. She'd tried and failed. And even worse? Now, she knew what—and who—she'd be missing.

The extra liquid in her eyes made the quaint town that served Glenmead College blur into an impressionist painting of greens and whites and blues. She cracked the window and shut her eyes against the breeze.

It didn't matter how happy she'd been, how much she'd enjoyed the professors' lectures, the camaraderie with her roommates and pals, or the freedom of being away from her family's expectations. It didn't matter that she'd finally felt at home somewhere. She knew that a huge part of that was because of Jeremy. He made her feel like she mattered. Like she was special and amazing. Like she belonged—just because she was her. Not because of her name.

Just then, the big clock in the bell tower chimed from behind them. Her time was up. It was everything she could do not to dissolve in tears and collapse to the floor of this vehicle. She bit hard on her lip again—fighting against herself.

They sped up the ramp toward the highway, accelerating toward a future that should be comfortable, but would be anything but for her.

"Darcy," her dad said as wind rushed through the back seat, "my papers."

She powered the window up, closing off the last two years. That was now her past. It was over.

1

—————

J eremy Walker had never felt his body strain viscerally in two different directions, until Darcy Hellston walked through his music club's door in the middle of the day with a briefcase. Opposing instincts warred. Stay, speak, beg—because *dammit*, he still wanted her. Avoid, hide, run—because Darcy was the only woman that held the power to crush him.

"Hi," she said. Darcy stepped forward, then back, then extended a hand halfway, then dropped it awkwardly.

Yeah, Jeremy thought, a real dilemma. You didn't shake with someone you'd shared mind-blowing sex with, and you sure as hell didn't hug someone you'd blown off. He stood stock-still.

She regrouped. "I'm glad to catch you here."

"What do you want?" He refused to play games with her.

Last he'd seen her, her light blond hair had been down and mussed from his hands. Now it was pulled back tight.

Much like the look in her hazel eyes, it shouted no nonsense. She sucked in a breath, her chest filling, shoulders shifting back. "I have a proposal for you. For Vine, that is."

Business? Really? He couldn't help a twitch of the eyebrow, which she must have taken as interest.

"I'd like to invest."

There went those diametrically opposed cells again. He was lucky his head didn't blow right off his shoulders.

And how the hell did she know that he needed a cash infusion for Vine? He'd put out feelers, he'd talked to a few people with connections—

Ah, their mutual friend Peter's wedding festivities. Someone must have told her. That sucked. He rubbed a hand over his face. He'd have preferred that the financial health of his venture remain private.

Darcy didn't wait for him to speak, just turned to the bar, pulled out a stool, and, despite the formfitting skirt and heels, hopped right up. Next thing he knew, she'd flipped open a leather folio that held an electronic tablet and propped it up. A swipe of her finger across the screen, and the words Hellston Enterprises showed up on a blue background.

She glanced over her shoulder. "Please sit." She pointed to the stool next to her.

"I've got a lot to do before opening," he said.

"I promise I won't take more than a few minutes of your time." She swiped again, and a large sum—more even than he needed—caught his eye at the bottom of a simple spreadsheet.

He chose the next stool over, leaving one in between—

a barricade to touching her. He crossed his arms over his chest and clenched his jaw.

"It's not unusual that small businesses incur more costs than expected during startup," she began, sliding the tablet closer to him. She spelled out her plan to buoy Vine's bottom line, and the numbers were sound. Actually, her terms were more than generous. Far more generous than the other offer he had on the table. And she hadn't been kidding; she was done with her pitch in no time. So fast, in fact, that he'd barely had time to think it through. It was straightforward, and he couldn't point out any holes in her logic or anything that should give him pause.

Only his instincts had serious misgivings about accepting Darcy's offer to invest in Vine. The club was *his*. And she was… Well, they had history. A history that was the polar opposite of the buttoned-up, briefcase-toting, all-business version of her that balanced precariously on his barstool in a pencil skirt and heels right now. Even her bare legs—reasonable, given that it was late August—which he'd been trying to keep his eyes off, didn't offset the prim appearance.

On the other hand, Vine needed this kind of cash infusion. The one offer he had was from a small startup group—in other words, a trio of pals that were looking to get in on the ground floor of something big. They didn't hold a candle to Hellston confidence-wise. Despite the fact that Vine was starting to gain traction in the Pittsburgh music scene, it was still very small potatoes as far as investors were concerned. He doubted he'd have a third offer. And he'd never have Hellston's interest if it wasn't for the personal connection with Darcy.

Darcy clasped her hands in her lap, yet she flipped the stylus over and over in her fingers. Her foot ticked up and down in an impatient rhythm. If her jitters were any indication, she was nervous. Did she have something at stake here, too? More than just a business deal?

Though he sat, his feet were planted firmly and he widened his stance. "What's in it for you?"

"The interest, of course," she said, looking at him like he'd missed the point.

"What else?"

"Helping small businesses can be really rewarding." She glanced away, then back. "I told you. You've got a good thing going. I believe if we build you a longer runway, you can really take off."

She wasn't telling him quite everything, he thought. But he also didn't sense that her reticence was anything sinister or sneaky. Maybe her business role simply required tight lips. Was he willing to take this money, to owe more money, to keep his dream alive, even without full disclosure from her?

She fumbled the stylus, recovered it, set it down next to her portfolio, then angled her shoulders toward him again.

Darcy opened her mouth at the same time he did, but he spoke first. "I have another offer. Why should I choose Hellston?"

For a second she froze, then her shoulders and hands both opened up. "Well, it's *Hellston*."

He rose from the stool and moved a few feet away. He put his hands on his hips and stared without seeing much.

"I'm happy to answer more questions," she said.

Jeremy remembered all the way back to their time together at Glenmead College when those same lips stretched in a wide, uninhibited laugh. She'd had a surprisingly good singing voice and often belted out lyrics without getting a single word wrong. The kind of girl who just had to dance if there was a band. Band or event t-shirts, cut-off shorts that highlighted her long, lean legs, flip-flops and a toe ring. And later, naked limbs and an enthusiastic, vocal lover who he'd find still burrowed into him when he woke. A friend and lover who was nearly always at his side—before she'd flaked out and disappeared on him, that was.

When he'd seen her at the wedding of one of their college roommates in True Springs a few months ago, it'd been awkward at first. He hadn't been nursing a grudge, but she'd showed her true colors when she vanished, and that had shifted things for him. Plus, she seemed so different from the young woman he remembered—all banker's wife or some shit, despite having no ring on her finger. She wore flattering, classy clothing, tame but clearly expensive jewelry, and a reserved demeanor he couldn't reconcile.

However, between the rehearsal dinner, the wedding, the celebratory vibe, and the free-flowing alcohol, she'd loosened up. So had he. They'd gravitated toward each other like they always had. Things had gotten hot. They'd spent a stunner of a night together—and then she'd crushed him. Again.

Only a few weeks ago, she'd shown up at one of Vine's pricier events. Of course he'd given her the event ticket in True Springs, but he was shocked as hell she'd used it.

After all, she'd made it clear she hadn't wanted to continue to see him. And that night at Vine? She'd stuck to that—hadn't even searched him out to say hello.

Except here she was again. In his club. Searching him out. Somehow—miraculously, uncannily, suspiciously—offering him exactly what he needed. Financially, anyway.

"So, what do you say?" she asked.

He turned back to her and saw she wore a polite smile. Her knees were pressed together, her ankles were crossed daintily, her hands sat clasped in her lap, and her back was straight.

Her demure, classy appearance didn't matter. If he took her up on this offer, it'd be like making a deal with the devil. It had taken him years to get over her after college, but that chance encounter in True Springs brought it home. She had been under his skin all that time, and having a taste of her made him want her in a big way all over again. He wished he could just flip a switch and turn it off, like killing the music from the club's sound system, but it wasn't that easy. Which sucked.

"I'll get back to you," he said.

Her shoulders dropped a fraction of an inch and a bit of light went out of her eyes. "You used to be the most decisive person I'd ever met."

This was a big flipping deal, as far as he was concerned. Big enough he wanted to roll it around awhile. He shrugged. "I'm not sure I want to be indebted to a woman who thinks George Michael is the be-all end-all."

Just like that, her eyes shone bright again, and a happy smile erupted. He felt a little like he'd gotten the wind knocked out of him. What had possessed him to reference that old, silly argument?

"So," she said, "should I—"

Jeremy spun and headed for the back. "I've got work to do."

She could forget the pushy sales tactics. He'd said he'd let her know, and he would. In his own time. In the meanwhile, she had found the door on the way in; she could surely find it on the way out.

———

Darcy huffed and then checked herself. She had to remember that this wasn't a cold call. She knew Jeremy well, or at least she had known Jeremy well. And intimately—but no, thoughts of him naked would derail her fast. She had to think more like a strategic businessperson with all her sales tactics lined up. Except she'd already kind of blown it.

She'd intended to explain that she wasn't here representing Hellston Investments, only Hellston Enterprises. But when he'd mentioned his other offer, she'd panicked and fallen back on the Hellston name. *Idiot,* she thought. *You should have prepared for that possibility.* This was what came of having no experience whatsoever to speak of... Damn.

She could chase after him, but he'd made it clear he was sparing her only the briefest amount of time and that he'd heard enough for today. She'd lost her chance—she'd have to save the information for another conversation.

Darcy worried her bottom lip. Had she sold him? Had she presented well? Was there anything else she should say? Any selling points she'd missed?

She had, she thought, been clear and concise about

what she could do for Vine, and the offer was definitely solid. If she'd already blown it, it was solely from inexperience. She'd given it her best shot, despite her complete lack of experience with preparing a pitch, sales tactics, and fielding questions.

She grimaced, then busied herself. She put her tablet to sleep and slipped it into its case along with the stylus, and then into the bag next to her.

She placed her hands down on the bar and nodded once. Jeremy hadn't said no flat out. She felt a bubble of hope, because that meant he was actually considering it. No matter the outcome, there wasn't any more to do here. But she would, with high hopes, prepare for a follow-up conversation.

Jeremy had always been straightforward. He didn't play games or mess around. If he liked you, he liked you. If he didn't, he didn't waste time on you. He knew right from wrong, straight talk from bullshit. And she wasn't kidding—he'd been pretty decisive. He knew what he wanted and, far as she knew, he didn't waffle. So, if he said he'd get back to her, he would.

She slid carefully off the stool, hefted the bag onto her shoulder, and then smoothed her hair. She'd gone for a professional look, slicking her hair back into a low bun. It was so tight that it almost gave her a headache. And these new pumps? She could now officially say that they sucked for walking on pavement *and* climbing on and off barstools.

Didn't matter, though. She'd needed to look as if she was an experienced professional, and more than anything, she wanted to be taken seriously.

She headed back down the hallway and exited Vine

onto Twenty-fifth Street. As she headed for her car, she realized she was practically smack in the middle of the Strip District. This neighborhood wasn't always pretty. In fact, there were parts that were rather ugly, sometimes stinky, and awfully noisy—especially these days between the hordes of people and the seemingly constant construction. And still, she thought as she soaked in the mix of old and new, rough and polished—she loved it. With all its character, it was so perfectly, uniquely Pittsburgh.

The hip Strip District—which was far outpacing downtown in terms of growth—was truly exploding. Many of the hot tech companies had a real presence in the Strip. New apartments and condominium complexes were constantly being built, and rents in the area had risen forty to fifty percent in the last five years alone. Everyone and their brothers wanted to live here. In a massive redevelopment effort, the old produce terminal—hundreds of thousands of square feet—had just been gutted to be converted into a food-centric mixed-use center. That meant even more housing, restaurants, night spots, artisan venues, retail shops, and office space.

So, for sure, the opportunities were here. And Darcy meant to be part of it—an essential part of it. She didn't care about the leading tech companies that had taken up residence or the huge new condominium developments. She wanted to help the older small business owners stay in place and keep up, and also help new ones get a foothold and thrive. It was those kinds of small independent places that made a neighborhood great.

Overall, people in the area were cognizant of keeping the area true to its roots, retaining the grittiness, while still making it a desirable place to live and work.

But money had a way of squeezing out heart. She would know.

And she didn't want that to happen to business owners like Jeremy. She believed in him. She always had.

The trick would be learning to believe in herself.

2

———————

When Jeremy got a call from his brother Jake to play some one-on-one basketball, he readily agreed. It might help get his mind off Darcy's offer—and Darcy. Jake picked him up, and luckily, with school in session, the court at the Robert E. Williams Memorial Park was unoccupied.

Unfortunately, his game was off. When his brother scored yet another basket and got set to defend, Jake asked, "So what are you gnawing on?"

Jeremy huffed out a breath—both annoyed that Jake could read him so easily and thrown because of the wording. They'd lost their dad not even six months ago. When faced with a decision or problem, Chuck Walker always said he had to "gnaw on it awhile." They all—Jeremy's mom Rita, he and Jake, and their youngest brother Jonah —were still very raw with missing him.

Jeremy drove, spun, shouldered his way past Jake, and managed to sink one. He retrieved the ball and swiped one arm over his forehead. "It's the club. I need more money."

"I'm surprised you aren't raking it in," Jake said. "It's packed every time I go."

Jeremy grimaced. "The space needed more work than I anticipated."

"Don't ever open a wall in an old building," Jake said. They both smiled, remembering Chuck's words when a project at their family's diner, the Wanderlust, had turned ugly.

"I've got some savings," Jake said.

"No, man," Jeremy said, "can't do it. Not from family. It's too much, too big. Besides, you and Sadie are just married with a new house to pay for."

Jeremy couldn't have been more psyched for his bro. As a longtime employee of the Wanderlust, Sadie had already been practically part of the family, and she and Jake were obviously nuts about each other. Even if the wedding was so rushed it seemed a little suspect, those two were proof that something real and true was possible.

For one night in True Springs, Jeremy had thought he might have a chance like that. He dribbled the ball with a little more force than necessary before he caught himself.

Jake said, "This house is a bargain compared to the loft I owned in Manhattan."

"But you and Sadie want to sink some cash into the diner, right?"

Jake nodded. "Yeah, but we're waiting until Mom comes back from her trip."

Jeremy chuckled. "Good plan." The Walker boys and Sadie had given Rita a major travel excursion for Mother's Day last year, and she'd be taking it in early spring. "No way can you make changes without her input."

"Exactly, and we don't want to rush the decisions or risk her bailing on her trip of a lifetime," Jake said, "so if you need—"

Jeremy shook his head and tossed the ball to Jake. "Hard no, but thanks."

They went a few more rounds before calling it quits.

Jake said, "So why not a loan?"

"Already got one of those at startup—part of the reason I'm not in the clear yet." Jeremy swigged from his water bottle, then said, "There's an investor who wants in." The fact that he'd said investor, singular, meant that yeah, Jeremy recognized that Darcy's offer was the only one worth considering.

"Nice," Jake said. "What kind? Vine's too small to catch the eye of a venture capitalist or angel investor."

Jeremy muttered, "Hardly an angel. Devil, maybe."

"Somebody you know?" Jake grabbed his towel and mopped his face and then his neck.

Jeremy blew out a breath. "Remember Darcy?"

"College Darcy? Broke-you-when-she-disappeared Darcy?"

Jeremy reared back. "That's harsh."

"Dude, you took it hard."

Jeremy rolled his eyes. That was the trouble with brothers when you were close. Even when you barely talked about shit, they just knew.

He and Darcy and six others had been roommates during his junior year at Glenmead College, a small liberal arts school with a great business program only an hour and a half from Pittsburgh. Needless to say, they'd shared a lot of alcohol and a lot of good times. He and Darcy had a tendency to end up kissing, and they became a solid duo without ever putting a name to it. For that one school year, everything was perfect.

Then, just ahead of summer break, Darcy disappeared without a word and stopped answering or returning his calls and texts. The next fall, some other girl showed up at the apartment in her spot after answering an ad. Jeremy had imagined an accident or some emotional tragedy. But nope, Darcy had just pulled a shit move. His status—boyfriend, friend with benefits, or bang-able roommate—apparently didn't matter enough to her to explain or say goodbye or anything.

Jeremy realized Jake was still waiting for an answer. "Yeah, that Darcy."

"So what?" Jake asked. "She just shows out of the blue? She's got money?"

Jeremy knew the questions would keep up if he didn't give his nosy bro some details. "I saw her at a wedding a few months ago, then more recently she showed up at Vine for an event, then boom—yesterday, out of the blue, she waltzed in with an offer." He shook his head. "Her family owns a big investment firm here in Pittsburgh. But as far as I can tell, they are more like financial investors. Huge funds and whatever. Doesn't seem like this is something they normally do."

Jake shrugged. "They could be branching out. Or maybe they just don't advertise the small-potatoes stuff."

Jeremy said, "She claims they like to support the community. Goodwill shit."

"So?" Jake asked.

Jeremy tossed the towel to the bench. "The terms seem a little too good to be true."

"She's probably trying to do you a solid. In the name of friendship, or maybe to make up for wigging out on you."

Jeremy said, "Who knows." He sure didn't. He'd been trying to figure out Darcy's motivations all night and had no answers.

Some young guys were lingering, obviously hoping to snag the court, so the brothers gathered up their stuff and headed for Jake's car.

Jake said, "Since we're already in uncomfortable territory, maybe now's a good time to pry details out of you about that True Springs comment you dropped at our reception."

Jeremy clenched his jaw and felt his shoulder blades pull tight. Damn. He'd known he was going to regret admitting he'd been to True Springs, drunk the supposedly magical water, and been kicked to the curb by true love. What exactly had he said to his brothers? Oh yeah, a cryptic comment implying that he was a True Springs reject.

"Let me guess," Jake said. "Darcy?"

"You sure are calling 'em today." Jeremy glared at his way-too-intuitive brother.

"Two for two, baby."

Jeremy muttered, "Three if we count hoops."

"True." Jake laughed and raised clasped hands as if he was a champion. They got in the car, and he blasted the air and returned to the question. "So, what the hell happened?"

Jeremy shifted in the passenger seat, trying to get comfortable. He really didn't want to talk about this—or even think about it. It was way too hot in this car. He powered down the window. But Jake still had the car in park.

Jeremy flipped his brother the bird, but Jake just grinned.

Jeremy shook his head. Finally, he said, "That wedding I mentioned? It was one of our roommates from Glenmead who got married recently, and all the festivities were there. I tried to avoid Darcy at first, but I don't know. There's something about her that always draws me in."

Something he'd never found with anyone else. Something fucking irresistible. Even this time around, when she seemed more serious, more subdued, a little uptight, or… maybe a little unhappy? Even after being burned by her before. Would he never learn?

Jake started the car and pulled out. "And?"

"And there was that town's stupid legend." Jeremy slid his brother a glance. "It put ideas in my head and things got heated."

"As in you fought? Or you got a room?"

He shut his eyes against the memory. "The latter." Heated was an understatement. He'd be forever scorched.

As a twenty-year-old, Darcy had been his dream girl. As a woman? The dream had been made real and fresh— the nearly ten years between only enhancing the impact. At a time in his life where—as a man, not a boy—he could truly appreciate it.

And he hadn't blown it up in his mind. They still had it —that extra-special magic they'd always had in bed and out. Except at True Springs, it'd been like she'd been starving. Like she'd been craving him all this time and couldn't get enough. Like she'd missed him, too. He hadn't expected it, given her newfound staid demeanor—but it'd been wild.

"So what?" Jake asked. "It ended badly?"

Jeremy's eye twitched. "You could say that."

3

———

Darcy and her friend Kalpani walked loose-limbed out of their usual Saturday morning yoga class at Exhale and headed by unspoken agreement for their favorite cafe, 21st Street Coffee and Tea. It was only a couple blocks over and practically right next to Darcy's condo on Fifth, and hot yoga meant iced coffees and sustenance. By the time the sweat dried, they'd be pulling on their sweatshirts and have devoured the breakfast sandwiches—and sometimes sweets—they always shared.

The eclectic, modern cafe was popular, with great choices and excellent coffee, but it was small and also invariably busy on a Saturday morning, so Darcy grabbed a table, while Kalpani went to order.

Darcy set her cell phone on the table where she could see it. She hadn't heard a peep from Jeremy, and it was killing her.

The two women had missed their midweek catch-up, so as soon as they started noshing, Kalpani updated Darcy on the latest drama at the salon where she was a stylist.

Soon enough, however, she leaned back in her chair and crossed her arms. "So, what was so important that you bailed on me last week? You said you were working on a project?"

Darcy couldn't help the smile that burst onto her face. "It was a pitch, basically. To invest in a small business in the Strip."

Kalpani raised an eyebrow. "Your dad asked you to do this?"

"God, no," Darcy said. And despite complete trust in Kalpani, Darcy didn't mention that she was sort of, kind of, not really, now borrowing the family business.

"Well then?"

"I came up with the idea on my own. Heard of a need and just decided to go for it." She grinned. She was so stoked about this—and yet so nervous that Jeremy would decline.

"Cool. Lord knows you need something to do with all that money you make," Kalpani said with a wink.

"That and I need something to do with my time," Darcy said. Something worthwhile, something she could be proud of, something she could call her own.

She glanced at her phone again, but it just sat there, silent and still.

Kalpani asked, "So what kind of business is it? How'd you hear about it?"

"It's a club—Vine."

"I've been there! That's, like, *the* place to hear new music."

And then Darcy didn't have to explain that she'd basically overheard Jeremy asking their friend Peter if he knew anyone interested in investing, because Kalpani suddenly sat up straight. Her eyes opened wide, her mouth formed an O, and she clasped her hands almost in yoga prayer position. "Oh," she said with clear sarcasm, "your dad's gonna love this."

Of all Darcy's friends, Kalpani knew only too well what parental pressure was like—albeit for different reasons. Darcy said, "What Daddy doesn't know won't hurt him."

"You go, girl," her friend said with a grin. "That place seems like it's doing well, though."

"You'd think so, given the talk," Darcy said. "But the owner needs more money to keep it going long enough to stay afloat and turn profit." For Kalpani's sake, Darcy explained in layman's terms about how a business's initial equity often wasn't enough and that growth equity could help them reach the next milestone.

Kalpani squinted at her. "You're really excited about this, aren't you?"

"I am," Darcy admitted. She had anticipation singing through her veins—a tingle of excitement that just buzzed. The underlying layer of nerves and doubt? Those she tried hard to ignore.

"He hasn't said yes yet, though."

"How'd you connect with the owner of Vine?" Kalpani took a hearty pull on her coffee.

"He's an old friend from college. I saw him recently at that wedding in True Springs."

"Wait a minute." Kalpani leaned forward and set her cup down with a thunk. "Is this the same guy that you got it on with?"

"Shh!" Darcy scanned the other tables—a lot of people knew her family, or at least of her family. She did not need juicy gossip getting back to them. "Keep your voice down. And how do you even know that? I never said that."

"You didn't have to. You were all stirred up when you got back. It was clear something big had happened."

Well, that was true, Darcy thought. Seeing Jeremy—being with Jeremy—had brought up all kinds of feelings she'd buried. It made her want. Want him, yes, but want *more*, too. It was an awakening the size of an avalanche—because, honestly, she'd stopped wanting things out of life a long time ago.

"So that brooding, tattooed hottie that owns Vine, huh?" Kalpani grinned. "Not exactly your usual."

He was all that and more with his dark hair, intense blue eyes, and lean frame, Darcy thought, but she said, "I don't have a usual, remember?" She stuck out her tongue at her friend. Kalpani was always pushing her to date, and Darcy was always avoiding it.

"Oh, sorry," Kalpani said. "Perhaps I should say, not the kind of guy your family would approve of?"

"I'm done seeking their approval anyway."

"Well, you're working on it."

Darcy sighed. Kalpani had known her a long time, and she wasn't wrong. Darcy tried. She'd come a long way. But her family made it really difficult to walk your own walk. And she hadn't had much worth pushing back against, until now. "This new venture is a big part of that," she said.

Kalpani nodded. "That's good. It really is." She took another little chunk of scone and then pushed the plate toward Darcy. "You think mixing business and sex is a good idea, though?"

Suddenly the indoor air felt cool on Darcy's arms, and

she wriggled into her long-sleeve pullover. "He's a good guy. If he takes me up on this offer, I don't think either of us will let it interfere. We were good friends once upon a time."

Kalpani frowned. "Be careful. Don't lose sight of the business end of things, and don't let him take advantage of you."

"I won't," Darcy said. But what she didn't tell Kalpani was that it was the other way around. To some degree, Darcy was taking advantage of him—or at least of Vine. Because she planned to cut her teeth on this, and then it would become a steppingstone. The first stop on her new path. Her own initial equity—in her future.

She peeked at her phone again. No notifications. It was unlikely Jeremy would call on a Sunday. Maybe tomorrow, she thought, as she sent another quick prayer out into the world for a yes.

In the long run, even if he declined, it wouldn't matter. It would take longer, but she was doing this. She'd find a way to identify other places that might need her. She would embrace this calling and run with it. She couldn't decide if she wanted to weep or cheer. Finally—only a few months ahead of her thirtieth birthday—she'd have a job. A career.

Yet she really, really wanted Vine to be her first. It had something special, something she desperately wanted to be part of.

She told herself it had nothing to do with the pull she felt toward Jeremy.

———

Jeremy sat on Vine's empty stage with his elbows on his knees. He looked at the special acoustical tiles he'd chosen, the metal barstools he'd gravitated to at first glance, the neon lighting he'd ordered to highlight the bar.

He could picture club goers clogging the bar area before they took to the dance floor, his bartenders hustling and grinning, his servers weaving with full trays. The faux-wood, nearly indestructible warehouse-style flooring he'd installed would hold up for endless nights of pumping bass and pounding feet.

Jeremy shook his head. It had been only a year and a half since he'd bought the property and started renovating, and he'd just celebrated a year since the grand opening. He had nearly everything he'd envisioned—except the money to pay better-known bands, advertise in a big way, and hire extra staff.

So close. So flipping close.

He was twenty-nine years old. He intended to head into his thirties with some serious upward momentum. Hell, he'd envisioned shooting out of a cannon. But he needed that cash to light the fuse. And he sure as hell hadn't sunk his heart and soul into the place to half-ass it now. No— cutting corners at this stage would mean the beginning of the end.

Unless he was missing something, Darcy's offer was some kind of godsend. The terms were more than reasonable—generous, even. From what she'd said, the deal could be sorted and finalized quickly. And the timing—not long after he'd decided to start making inquiries—had made him feel like the universe was on his side.

Like he'd told Jake, perhaps too good to be true. Or it could just be a sweet deal at the right time.

The only red flag was Darcy herself. Beyond the question of whether he could trust her, Jeremy didn't want to be beholden to her or her company. He didn't want to have to communicate with her regularly, or even infrequently. He didn't want to be constantly hammered with the fact that he couldn't have her and shouldn't want her.

He'd been thinking about her even before this offer. Truth be told, he'd been thinking about her nonstop since that encounter in True Springs. Hell—her smile had been like a punch to the gut, her taste had been like revisiting heaven, and the way she'd felt under him and responded to him? Man, he'd felt like a king.

And yet—when she'd balked at seeing him again? He'd crashed—barely feeling like a life form, let alone royalty.

And yeah, goddammit, for all he looked tough, he could be as romantic or maudlin as the next guy. And Darcy Hellston seemed to ramp up that factor exponentially—even now that he was a friggin' grown man.

She'd left a voicemail on his phone yesterday. No surprise, given it'd been a week and a half since she'd proposed this idea, and yet it had thrown him because they hadn't exchanged numbers that night in True Springs. She'd kept her message short and to the point. *I'm checking in regarding my offer to invest in Vine. Let me know if I can answer any questions to help you reach a decision.*

Completely businesslike, but he didn't like the way his body thrummed at simply hearing her voice. The number still sat in his recent calls, along with the voicemail. If he said yes, he'd have to enter her name and save it into his contacts list.

Unable to sit still any longer, he got up and went behind the bar. It was Saturday of Labor Day weekend, and he wasn't sure what to expect. Tonight's band, Hijinx, usually drew a decent crowd. But holidays were unpredictable. They could be mobbed because people had extra time or dead because people were having barbecues or escaping for the weekend. The staff wasn't due for about another half-hour, but he'd check inventory, haul kegs, whatever it took to keep from texting Darcy and taking her up on her offer.

4

———————

By Tuesday afternoon, Jeremy couldn't stand it any longer. The Hellston agreement Darcy had presented was hands-down better than the one Peter's connection had offered, and it was a far bigger, more reputable company. Going with a startup could be dicey—what if they themselves found themselves in trouble? What if they reneged? What if they pulled a fast one from inexperience or desperation or impatience?

The plain fact of the matter was that he was only putting off accepting the Hellston offer because of Darcy. And yet it was Darcy who'd likely driven the deal.

Time to man up. In this case, that meant he'd have to ignore his ego, turn his heart to stone, and put his libido in deep freeze. He could handle that, right?

Darcy picked up on the first ring. "This is Darcy."

"Hi, it's Jeremy."

"Oh, hi," she said. "Hold on a second." Wherever she'd been, the background noise abruptly ceased. Another couple of seconds passed before she spoke again. "Have you made a decision?"

Perfect. All business. Just what he was hoping for. "I have. Let's get it done."

"Great!" she said.

Jeremy frowned at the exuberance in her voice.

"I'm so—" She cleared her throat. "I assume you'd like to proceed as soon as possible?"

"Yeah," he said, "but I'll need to review the paperwork."

"Yes, of course. I just wanted to get a sense of your needs in terms of time frame. I'll have legal draw them up first thing tomorrow. Are you okay with signing electronically, or do you want me to bring them by?"

An urge to see her again erupted as quickly as the burst of flame from a lighter, and Jeremy clenched his jaw. "Electronically is cool." There was no reason to meet. She'd only distract him, and he needed to pay extra-close attention to the fine print.

She took down his email address, then said, "Thanks for partnering with me. I look forward to helping Vine reach its maximum potential."

Excellent. Polite and professional, Jeremy thought. Just the way he wanted to keep things. Why, then, did he feel disappointed?

———

Darcy sat down to work in her home office, but when she glanced at her email, something caught her eye.

She sat up straight. An email from Jeremy. She read

the first line carefully, then moved to the bottom and read that line. He'd reviewed the documents and…

Her heart was pounding, and it wasn't long, but she was careful to take her time anyway…making sure…but… yes…his answer was yes!

Oh my God. She'd been so worried that he would change his mind and back out. But he'd looked through all the paperwork she'd sent—and he was *still* on board! Which meant she was truly in business!

It was shocking, and yet she'd been as prepared as she could be for this scenario. She'd already set up a new, dedicated account and had transferred in a hefty sum. She'd hired Esther Saulman, an attorney well versed in contracts of this kind, and they'd worked fast to get a basic Hellston Enterprises agreement prepared before she'd even brought the proposal to Jeremy. Esther had also advised Darcy on registering her new business name. Because Hellston was her legal name, too, not just her father's, there was no infringement.

Using the family's business office address without permission wasn't exactly kosher, however. The advisor urged her to work out something official—maybe renting a small suite of offices from the company. Darcy had promised she would—but she was dreading speaking with her father enough to drag her feet. She didn't want to tell him what she was up to. Didn't want his opinions, advice, or strong-arming. Most certainly didn't want to hand him any ammunition that could puncture her sails—emotionally or practically speaking.

Darcy double-clicked open the email and scooted her chair closer to take the time to read Jeremy's message all the way through. At the end, she flopped back in her chair and covered her heart with one hand.

Yes.

She was wowed and grateful, excited and terrified. Not only were her emotions on overdrive, her brain was, too, as she thought back over all the decisions she'd made thus far.

She did need to speak with her father, but Darcy figured she could get away with the borrowed address for a little while. Heck, for all anybody knew, Hellston Enterprises was an offshoot sanctioned by Hellston Investments. She'd gone so far as to play into that angle, when she'd panicked at Jeremy's questioning during the pitch. But her reaction had been legit—she herself pretty much had a Hellston fortune, which meant there was no way she'd default on the agreement. Plus, using her father's business address temporarily was safe and expedient: she avoided using her home address on a business filing, and she didn't have to hold up Vine's deal in order to find office space. It'd be a waste anyway.

Much like the hours she spent managing her many investments, she'd work from her home office. She liked her peace and quiet, and she was largely happy to avoid dealing with people. She had an ergonomic chair and keyboard, two huge monitors, a u-shaped desk where she could lay out as many papers and reference materials as she liked, music if she felt like it, and a big window with a gorgeous view of the city.

She swiveled in her chair and looked out at the sunlight winking on the buildings, then the water and bridges that were almost always visible from anywhere in Pittsburgh.

Glorious possibility filled her. Yes, indeed, she loved her view.

Darcy spun back to the computer, intending to print Jeremy's email. In the browser, however, she realized she had another important email—from the electronic signature program. Darcy's blood thrummed. That meant…

He'd signed!

Jeremy's yes was in writing! He'd really, truly, actually, for-real signed!

She clicked open the email, then the document, and hit print. She popped out of her chair and bounced up and down in time with the chugging of the printer.

She snatched each page up as it came out, checking each spot he'd needed to initial or sign.

When she had them all, she whooped and did a little happy dance.

She was more excited about this than anything—truly anything—that had happened in years. Maybe ever.

She shouted, "Yes!" Then she dropped into her chair, clutched the papers close, and grinned from ear to ear.

"Darcy? Everything okay?"

Darcy scooted her chair so she could see past her monitors to her housekeeper, Ingrid. "Everything's great," she said. "Better than great."

"Your offer? It's a done deal?" Ingrid held her arms up in a victory pose even though she held a duster in one hand.

"Yes!" Darcy jumped up and crossed the room. She held the papers out and pointed to Jeremy's signature. "He signed! It's really happening!"

Ingrid hugged her and then held her at arm's length. "I knew it! I told you not to doubt! You're the hardest-working person I've ever worked for—and I have worked for some *very* successful people. You're smart *and* you've obviously got the Hellston head for business."

"Thank you for believing in me." Darcy pulled Ingrid tight for another quick hug, her heart swimming with love for this woman. "I can't wait to get to work."

"Why am I not surprised?" Ingrid chuckled. "Just don't work too hard. It's beautiful outside."

"I won't." Like Kalpani, Ingrid was pushing Darcy to get out more. "Thanks for checking on me."

Darcy's parents insisted she have someone take care of the house and do the cleaning, but in turn Darcy insisted the older woman come only two days a week. Because, honestly, there wasn't that much that needed done. Darcy lived alone, she never entertained, and she was tidy by nature. Still, it was nice to have company sometimes. Especially Ingrid's company, because she'd been a fixture for so long that she was more like an aunt than an employee. And when Ingrid's blood pressure got out of hand or she had worries about her children and grandchildren, it gave Darcy someone to look after, too.

Darcy tapped the papers into a neat stack, then settled in with a pencil to read carefully through every word again.

When she felt satisfied, she took a deep breath and turned to the computer to add her own electronic signature and initials.

She hit print once more, marveling at the fully executed pages. All because she'd reconnected with Jeremy in True Springs and had decided to use that special event ticket he'd left.

Her new venture, Hellston Enterprises, was officially

underway. She—Darcy Hellston, college dropout and family embarrassment—had created a new beginning, a career, a future.

———

Darcy couldn't help herself. Even though Jeremy had said email was fine, she decided to hand-deliver the fully executed contract.

She wanted to use the glossy folders she'd rush ordered last week. They bore the words Hellston Enterprises. No logo, just the classy type treatment that matched what she'd done as a header on the documentation and in her email signature. Included in the navy and white packet was Vine's contract, a confirmation of the electronic payment setup, and some disclosures that Esther had insisted on.

This was momentous. And Darcy was determined to eke every bit of thrilling joy out of it that she could.

Vine's front door was locked. Darcy knocked, then pounded, but no one answered. It was only a couple of hours before opening, and she'd assumed Jeremy would be here prepping. She probably should have called first, or maybe just texted.

Darcy headed for Mulberry Way, sure there must be a back entrance from the alley. Her pumps, navy-blue skirt, and classic white blouse weren't exactly alley material, but that was okay.

A door was propped open with a keg. Darcy leaned around some wooden pallets to check. Sure enough, the door bore Vine's logo.

She poked her head into the dark hallway and called, "Hello?"

Again, no response.

She thought about leaving and calling Jeremy to schedule a time, then shook her head. No, she was here. She was doing this. And if it was only someone from his staff who'd propped this door open, then she'd simply come back again tomorrow.

Her heels clopping on the planks of the old wooden floor sounded loud and out of place, so she switched to a tiptoe walk. Pittsburgh's Strip District had once been mainly warehouses and markets. In the last handful of years, gentrification had been rampant, but thankfully, most owners and city officials felt keeping the character of the Strip intact was a priority. Jeremy must too, because Vine had hardwood floors and exposed brick walls.

A few doors opened off the hallway, but they looked like storage rooms. Up ahead, another door was propped open, and she thought it must go to the main club area. Light spilled from yet another room just before that on the right, and Darcy braced herself to see Jeremy again. She was nervous—wanting desperately to see him, yet knowing he likely didn't want to see her.

She shifted her bag up on her shoulder and smoothed her skirt as she approached.

The room was small and square, with red brick walls and an understated bronze linear chandelier over a big plank-style desk. Jeremy wasn't there, but it was definitely his office. Papers littered every surface, and she wondered if anything ever got filed in the filing cabinet on the back wall. There was a mini fridge and a wooden cupboard, on top of which sat a Keurig coffee maker, some discarded mugs and silverware, a few boxes of coffee pods, and a stack of papers. A small printer sat on the floor, within arm's reach of an old wooden chair—the kind that would tilt backward and swivel, too.

Very male, she thought, and the anticipation about seeing Jeremy ramped up another notch. Darcy swallowed hard as she continued on.

When she stepped into the main room of the club, she was struck by how different the space looked with the lights up and no bodies. There was a wide expanse of new flooring, a stone wall behind an oddly empty stage, and a stretch of dark bar, and the remaining two walls were brick with a shallow, chest-high counter to set down drinks. She hadn't paid much attention that day she'd came to make the offer—she'd been consumed by nerves and trying hard to ignore what sitting two feet away from Jeremy was doing to her.

She crossed the space and headed for the bar, this time letting her heels make noise. Jeremy had disappeared behind the door on the other side of the bar last time, and it might be best if some noise announced her presence.

Sure enough—he appeared in the doorway, then froze when he spotted her.

She seized the strap of her bag like a lifeline, but kept moving toward him as she scrambled for an icebreaker. "I tried the front. No one answered."

"Because we're not open," he said, and his lips flattened.

But his expression didn't matter to her. Scowling his displeasure or smiling with satisfaction after an orgasm that had rocked them both—dear God, why did her brain flash to those things—he was the hottest man she'd ever seen. She'd always been drawn to his rough edges and intensity. Was it because she'd been raised amongst the pampered, preppy elite and opposites attracted? Or was it simply a chemical thing?

"That's the point. I didn't want to bother you when you were busy," she said. "I brought you copies of the agreement."

"You could have sent them via email," he said, but took a step forward.

"I did that, too," she replied, and did the same. "I don't know about you, but I like my paper." She shifted her leather satchel enough to pull out his folder.

One more step forward, and she handed him the folder with a smile. Something crossed his face, but Darcy couldn't decipher it. Maybe it was better not to.

He thanked her and let the folder dangle from one hand at his side.

"You're welcome. My pleasure." Then she added, "Congratulations," and extended her hand to shake his.

Bad idea. Because the second his palm touched hers, she felt it again. *It*—that undeniable something that always occurred when she touched him.

One pump of their joined hands and he broke the contact with a curt nod—yet he held her eyes. The moment stretched. She felt that pull, a yearning deep down, a quickening—

Jeremy cleared his throat. "Just so you know, despite..." His free hand had fisted, before he waved the folder between them. "This will remain strictly professional."

Darcy took a deep breath and nodded. She understood.

She'd hurt him, and he wasn't going to give her another chance.

She hurt, too—every time she thought back to that night in True Springs. Once she'd let her walls down, they'd shared the most amazing night. Laughing, teasing, touching. And the actual sex? My God, it was like the whole city of Pittsburgh's over-the-top fireworks display had gone off in her body. It might have been because she hadn't had sex in so many years, but more likely it was because it was Jeremy.

Regardless, her mind had been just as rocked as her body. So early in the morning when her brain was short on sleep and overwhelmed on endorphins, when Jeremy suggested that he'd like to see her back home? She had panicked. Her eyes had become saucers, her body had tensed, and her throat had locked up. She'd never learned confidence, and she often froze up if she was put on the spot. She'd spent so many years second-guessing herself and fearing big misunderstandings that freezing up had almost become a default.

She had assumed she and Jeremy were having a one-night stand, seizing the moment, taking advantage of being away from real life. And she flashed back to how brutal it'd been when she made the terrible decision to cut him out of her life. He'd had his pants on before she'd begun to process. And after he'd slammed the door, she sobbed her heart out, considering what Jeremy's question could have meant, what a different reaction could have led to as two mature, single adults.

She'd give almost anything to take that moment back. To have answered with something flirty. To have simply said *yes*.

Yet would she have ended up here, with this shiny new venture and bright future if it hadn't gone down like that? Darcy gave herself a mental shake. What was done was done. And now, they'd entered a whole different kind of relationship.

"Of course," she said, straightening her shoulders a touch. "I've already generated the first payment. It should hit your account in two days max."

"Thanks," he said.

"No problem." There was so much she wished she could say, so much she'd like to express. But she'd lost that chance in True Springs, and now they'd entered into a situation where emotions had no place. She had to remember that to Jeremy, this was only a simple business transaction, a necessary evil. "I'm pleased to help."

She spun to go. He'd never know how pleased, how grateful, how important this was to her. Or how sorry she was that she'd missed the chance to see what could have been between them.

Jeremy's footfalls sounded behind her. "I'll open the front door for you," he said.

"No need," she said. "Easy enough to go out the way I came in." She began to cross the dance floor. When she turned to glance at him, she realized he was right behind her. Her heart beat faster, but she only said, "Good luck."

Her feet carried her forward, yet the urge to take one more peek was strong. She half turned with a little wave.

Jeremy stood—arms crossed over a black t-shirt and jean-clad legs planted wide in the middle of the floor— watching her.

She raised a hand in an abbreviated wave. "Let me know if you need anything else."

He wouldn't. He didn't want her anymore. Not for anything but her money.

Trouble was, she very much still wanted him.

5

____

Friday night arrived and Vine was hopping. In fact, Jeremy figured they were probably nearing capacity and decided it was about time to check in with tonight's bouncers, Steve and Alberto. Instead of squeezing through the log-jammed bar area and then the entry against the flow of traffic, he headed for the back so he could cut through the alley and come around. As soon as he stepped out the door, he could hear the chatter from around front even over the thump of the music coming from inside. And when he rounded the corner, he really got a thrill—loads of people.

Jeremy ducked under the rope next to Alberto, who was collecting cover charges and manning the clicker that counted entries. He asked, "Where are we?"

Alberto grinned. "One hundred thirty-three."

"Cool. One in, one out at one-forty-five," Jeremy reminded him. Maximum capacity was one hundred and fifty bodies, but he didn't like to push it. Most of this line wouldn't get in anytime soon.

"On it," Alberto said. Then he separated a large stack from the wad of cash he held and handed it to Jeremy with a wink.

As Jeremy wrapped his fingers around it, he nodded with satisfaction. A full-capacity night was a good night.

They hit those often, but Jeremy wanted every night to qualify. As soon as Darcy's cash hit Vine's account, he'd up the advertising dollars. Weekends were nearly always winners. Thursdays were usually decent. But he'd love to increase traffic on Wednesdays. So far they were closed Sundays through Tuesdays. Not enough people came out those nights, so it didn't make sense to pay bands and staff.

Jeremy clapped Alberto on the back and turned toward the open-door vestibule to check on Steve, who was doing the carding. He raised his chin, and Steve called over the noise, "Six."

Jeremy gave Steve a thumbs-up. Six fake IDs tonight. Hopefully that lot would be back when they turned twenty-one—or at least got better fakes. His guys were well trained, though. They'd been with him since day one.

When Jeremy turned back to Alberto, he immediately zeroed in on a head of straight, pale blond hair, which quickly ducked behind someone else in line. There wasn't a doubt in his mind that it was Darcy—and only a split second of seeing her and his pulse quickened. What was wrong with him?

And what the hell was she doing here? Checking the club out on the sly? Info gathering? She'd already made her offer, and he'd already signed, so what did it matter?

He clenched his teeth. She was about nine deep, maybe. She'd make it in. Whatever—he had nothing to hide.

Alberto took the cover charge from the next guy in line and added it to his roll of cash. Jeremy put his hand on the bouncer's shoulder, leaning in so that Alberto could hear him but the club goers in line couldn't. "About nine back. The blonde with the big sliver earrings in a black top."

"That's every woman here," Alberto shot back.

"You'll know her," Jeremy said. "Not fake blond, but real and nearly towhead. A class act. A little out of place. Her name is Darcy. She doesn't pay."

"You got it, boss," Alberto said.

———

As soon as Dog Daze finished the set, Jeremy handed each of the sweaty, grinning band members a beer. He shook hands, clapped shoulders, and thanked them. They were an up-and-coming local band somewhere between grunge and blues who brought some major enthusiasm every time they played. People turned out in force, and Jeremy fully expected them to hit it big one of these days.

Jeremy was congratulating them on a new song that the crowd had seemed to love, when, out of the corner of his eye, he caught a flash of lightness in the midst of all the dim lighting. Darcy was inside and nearby.

"I'll send another round and some waters, too," he told the band, and held the door open for them to the green room—nothing fancy, and not green, but definitely a space bands could chill out in between sets.

When he turned, he found Darcy weaving deter- minedly through people to get to him. A dark-haired woman wearing a slightly bemused expression trailed her. He moved to a slightly more open spot.

Darcy nearly barreled into his chest, and she looked steamed. "You didn't have to do that."

"Do what?" he asked. His annoyance level at her even being here didn't lend itself to cooperation.

"Let us in for free."

Good, Jeremy thought, Alberto had extended his direction to include Darcy's pal, just as he would have done.

"Yes, I did," he said. Because no way. He wasn't doing this with her. Whatever she was—ex-college girlfriend, recent one-night stand, or current business partner—she didn't get to do the I-have-more-money thing with him. He might have needed a sizable loan for the club, but he could sure as hell afford to treat a woman or two to a measly cover charge.

"It's perfectly reasonable that I should pay like any other person walking in off the street."

"As of Tuesday, when I signed my name to Hellston's dotted line," he said, "you're not just anybody."

"Jeremy—"

"You've already paid, Darcy," he said. He could blame the harsh tone on trying to speak over the noise, but the fact was that he was a little bitter. He didn't really want her to have a vested interest in his place. He *really* didn't want her showing up all the time.

She scowled and put her hands on her hips. Christ. She wore tight leather pants that showed every damn curve. And the position drew her ultra-fine breasts to his attention, too. They looked a little more generous than in True Springs, and he ached to see what had to be a sexy push-up bra against all that softness.

He turned to go but stopped when she grabbed his forearm. He looked at her fine-boned hand on his arm. Any time they were skin on skin, it was…

He tore his gaze up to scowl at her.

She dropped her hand. "Let me introduce you to my friend." She half turned, indicating the petite woman who still appeared to be amused by this situation, given the smirk on her face. "Jeremy, this is Kalpani. Kalpani, this is Jeremy."

"Hi," he said, and shook Kalpani's hand.

"Nice to meet you," Kalpani said, and now her dark eyes narrowed. Was she sizing him up or delivering a warning?

Jeremy didn't give a shit if he'd been rude, and he definitely didn't want to think about what Darcy might have told her pal. "I've got things to do," he told the duo. "Your drinks are on the house."

Darcy huffed out a breath—again that tight black top over those luscious breasts.

"If you don't like it," he said, "tip generously."

Jeremy turned, skirted the far end of the bar, and pointed out Darcy and Kalpani to one of his bartenders He felt Darcy's gaze on him the whole while.

Christ, it was going to be a long night.

6

———

Darcy had returned solo to Vine again on Saturday night, hoping to squeak in under Jeremy's radar, except the bouncer remembered her. Of course, he still didn't let her pay the cover charge. She didn't see Jeremy, however, and slipped through the crowd to a spot along the back wall to watch the band.

Not ten minutes later, however, she'd felt Jeremy's eyes on her. And only a few minutes after that, a server delivered her a drink. Vodka tonic, double lime. The bartender had also remembered, or maybe Jeremy had.

Regardless, it was obvious that there was no way she was slipping into Vine unnoticed. So the next Friday—her third evening visit to Vine as a patron since she became an investor—Darcy didn't bother keeping a low profile. She went straight to the bar. Jeremy could scowl all he wanted.

As she sipped slowly on her drink and watched the band, the crowd, the staff, the flow, she was thinking hard about what seemed to be working well for Vine. Likewise, where improvements could be made, what might increase traffic, and what other options Jeremy might consider. It was the most fun she'd had in ages.

Total bonus: she loved live music. She'd forgotten how much. Without Kalpani at her side, she didn't feel all that comfortable dancing, but she enjoyed just watching and listening. So far, every band she'd seen at Vine had had its own sound. Tonight was a group she'd never heard of called Blue Bass. She'd expected blues music, and certainly there was an underlying soulful vibe, but the tunes were some sort of upbeat funk with lyrics the crowd seemed to love to shout out.

The people watching was also a blast. Vine attracted a far more interesting mix than her country club, or even her yoga classes. Maybe she didn't quite fit in here, but with such a diverse group, no one paid her much mind, which she quite liked.

Truth be told, she had never felt she fit well in her own world either.

Eventually, Darcy spun on her stool and pushed her empty vodka tonic glass forward. The bartender was a woman close to her own age with black hair and all kinds of piercings and tattoos, who, so far, anyway, always wore a black Vine t-shirt with the sleeves ripped off. She finished an order and came right over to Darcy even though they were really busy.

"Seltzer?" the bartender asked. She'd obviously caught on that Darcy limited herself to one alcoholic drink. At least out and about like this. Overdoing it at Peter's wedding was an anomaly and had had far more to do with getting drunk on Jeremy.

"Yes, please," Darcy said, straining to be heard.

In no time at all, a seltzer with double lime—this woman really was good—appeared in front of her.

"What's your name?"

"Raven," the bartender said.

Darcy smiled. The name fit. "Thanks, Raven."

"No problem, Darcy. My treat," Raven said with a wink.

Darcy laughed. Because they'd been through the song and dance already. The staff was under strict instructions not to let her pay for drinks, even soda. But as Jeremy had suggested, Darcy made up for the special attention by tipping well.

Right now, he was at the other end of the bar, slinging drinks every bit as fast—maybe faster—than his staff, and she couldn't help but sneak a glance. Even when she was entranced with the music, Darcy always knew where he was. She felt his presence like a sixth sense. Not that he'd try to sneak up on her or anything. Actually, he seemed determined to keep his distance. Darcy sighed and turned back to the band.

The couple next to her got up to dance and two guys took their seats. The one closest to her gave her a once-over. She ignored him.

When the band took a break, she turned back to the bar.

"Can I buy you a drink?"

"No, thanks," Darcy said. She smiled and inclined her head toward her glass, which was still quite full.

"Oh, come on, that doesn't look strong enough for a Friday night." He was a bull of a man—short and stocky but pumped up. Not a problem in itself, but his slimy grin did spell trouble—or at least annoyance for her.

"It's just the way I like it," Darcy said. For all he knew, it was half vodka.

"Good band, huh?"

"Yes," she said.

"Have you heard them before?" he asked.

She shook her head. Poor guy was trying really hard to make conversation, but Darcy had interest in only one man—Jeremy. No matter that the shoulder he'd been throwing her was as cold as the one she was trying to give this guy.

She grabbed her glass and slid off the stool. "Excuse me." In her experience, if you gave a guy already working it a single inch, he'd try for a mile. She headed back along the bar toward the restrooms.

Luckily, there was a nice, long line, and by the time she got out, the band had started up again. There was a spot—just spacious enough for one—along the far wall.

She picked her way through the crowd on the dark dance floor and was nearly there when a hand wrapped around her upper arm. She spun and came face to face with that same slimy smile.

"Hey"—he leaned in too close, talking loud to be heard over the band—"I saved your seat." He tugged and made to go.

She dug in her feet and pulled her arm the opposite direction. "I'm done sitting."

Slimy grinned. "You want to dance? I'm down with that."

She shook her head. "Find another partner."

Just then, Jeremy appeared looking like hell bearing down. A myriad of emotions careened through her, as he clapped a hand hard on the guy's shoulder. "You heard the lady."

"Fuck off," Slimy said. He knocked Jeremy's arm away as he spun around. Darcy braced herself, afraid a fight would ensue. But Slimy either recognized Jeremy as Vine's owner or got a really good look at Jeremy's expression, because he raised his hands and took a step back. Just in time, Darcy sidestepped to avoid a crushed toe.

"She was alone," Slimy said. "I was just trying to keep her company."

"You even speak to her again, you're out," Jeremy said.

"Whatever, asshole," Slimy said. He drove his shoulder into Jeremy's as he stormed away, but thankfully, Jeremy let that go.

Instead, he scowled at Darcy.

"What's that look for?" she asked.

"Come with me," he growled, and grabbed her arm.

She twisted her arm up and away, breaking his hold. "Don't even."

A pained look crossed his face.

Lights flashed, music pumped, moving bodies gyrated around them. They stared at each other for at least three beats of the music.

"Please," Jeremy said.

She inclined her head a fraction of an inch, then shut her eyes for a second. When she opened them, he'd turned, barreling off through the crowd.

She threw up her free hand, leaned over to discard her seltzer on the ledge, and then hustled to follow in his wake.

———

Jeremy pushed open the door marked "Private" and prayed Darcy was right behind him. He hadn't meant to grab her —*Jesus*. He'd just needed her out of there. He needed her safe. And he needed to be able to speak with her without yelling.

When he saw that shithead bothering her, Jeremy had had to grit his teeth and bear it. When it became clear the fucker wasn't listening to her signals, Jeremy had worked his way down the bar just in case. He'd been relieved when she slipped away. Then next thing he knew, the jerk was on the move.

When the guy grabbed her? Christ, Jeremy had nearly gone through the roof. It'd taken everything he had not to swing first and speak his piece later.

Jeremy jammed the key in the lock to his office and shoved open the door. By the time he turned, Darcy was standing behind him.

She crossed her arms over her chest. "You didn't have to do that." He opened his mouth to apologize for manhandling her, but she said, "I had it under control."

Oh, *that*. He scoffed. "Yeah, right."

"I did."

He put his hands over his eyes and raised his face to the ceiling. "Guys like that—"

"I've encountered plenty of guys like that."

God help him, this night was getting worse and worse. Jeremy shook his head. She dealt with these jackasses regularly? Christ almighty, he was going to have to change the carding system. Legal drinking age, but a blatant asshole? Sorry. No entry.

Jeremy said, "Then you know those kinds of shitheads

think a woman alone is out on the town for one reason only."

She pursed her lips and her nostrils flared.

"Hold up—I'm not saying it's fair. I'm just saying that crap still happens. I see it nearly every fucking time we're open."

She blew out a breath.

Jeremy said, "Are you going to keep showing up here?"

"For a while, at least," she said.

What? When I start turning a profit you'll stop coming? That thought crossed his mind, but right now he was far more concerned about avoiding repeats of what just happened. He took a breath as if it was a lungful of patience. "Can't you bring your friend with you? Kalpani, right?"

"She's been busy."

"Another friend? Anybody?"

Darcy frowned.

"It's your call. You're a grown woman." He was at a loss. "Just…if you're alone, could you try not to come in looking like that?"

"Like what?" She threw out her arms. "I've got more clothes on than half the people here!"

In terms of actual skin showing, that was true. He scrubbed both hands over his face again. But those leather pants. They practically screamed *fuck me*. He should know—all he could think of when he saw them was—

No—that line of thought was not going to help here.

"It's so—" What in the hell could he even say?

"So what, Jeremy? I don't get it." She huffed out a

breath, making her chest heave. "You're going to have to actually spit it out. I can't read your mind."

Her top tonight was sort of shimmery—some mix of black and silver. It had short sleeves; it wasn't even tight. But those pants hugged every sexy curve from her hips to her calves. He gestured lamely at her lower half.

"Most of the women in here have half their butt cheeks hanging out of their skirts!" She stamped a foot—a black super-high heel. "What is wrong with my outfit?"

"Those pants! They're too fucking sexy!" he said.

Darcy's eyes widened and her mouth dropped open.

Christ. Now he'd gone and made a worse mess. Jeremy's eye twitched. He looked at the ceiling again and then back at Darcy. Okay, okay, he could admit it. "On you, they are too fucking sexy." Anything to get her to stop wearing them to his club.

A dangerous light stole into her eyes. "You like them," she said, and moved toward him.

He held up a hand.

She hesitated. Then her shoulders dropped, and she nodded. "Fine. I won't wear the pants again. At least not here."

God help him. He hated the idea of her wearing them elsewhere even more.

What was it about this woman? Why couldn't he ignore her? Force her out of his mind? Banish her from his dreams? He crossed his arms over his chest.

"Are we done?" she asked.

Jeremy inclined his head, and yet he knew he'd never ever been *done* when it came to Darcy.

She spun—those pants, those sexy heels, that stunning blond hair—and marched out of his office.

Jeremy took a moment to try to calm the hell down, then followed, making sure to lock his office door behind him. When he yanked open the door to the dance floor, he couldn't help it—he scanned the crowd for Darcy.

And just in time, he saw it like it played out on a screen—every single frame in Technicolor—and yet had no way to stop it. One wild dancer crashed into a server with a full tray. Drinks went airborne and then crashed to the floor. Liquid splashed and spread.

And Darcy's momentum, coupled with her precarious footwear, meant she didn't have a chance. Those heels flew out from under her, and her head smacked the floor so hard that Jeremy swore he heard it over the music.

He leapt forward, and a few people near Darcy crouched down to help, but most of the crowd hadn't seen. Ensconced in their own worlds, they jumped and danced. Jesus—she'd get trampled.

Rather than try to control the crowd, Jeremy scooped her up and hefted her into a fireman's carry. Deadweight. *Unconscious.* Jeremy barreled for the private door again, fumbled one-handed with his key, and burst into his office. He set her on the desk, holding her up, one hand cradling her head. Her eyes were shut, and a sick feeling washed over him.

Raven flew in behind him and flipped the lights on. "Here," she said, and laid a folded bar towel on the desk. She had the first-aid kit, too. Carefully, he lowered Darcy onto the desk—right over all his papers—and adjusted her head on the towel. When he pulled his hand away, it was bloody.

"Fuck," he whispered.

"Mara is bringing ice," Raven said. "Should I call 911?"

"Either that or I'm driving her to the—"

Darcy's eyes fluttered and a look of pain crossed her features.

Jeremy didn't even realize he'd been holding his breath, until it whooshed out.

She groaned and raised a hand to her head.

"Careful," he said.

Darcy blinked, squinting at the lighting that hung over the desk. Mara, one of the servers, came in with a bag of ice and another towel.

"Can you sit up?" Raven asked Darcy. "I want to see that bump."

She levered herself up slowly, making sure she wasn't tall enough to hit the linear lighting above her, and Jeremy supported her back in case she got woozy.

"Wow, that hurts," Darcy said, but she sat under her own power, and Jeremy began to breathe a little easier.

Raven moved behind Darcy. Again, Darcy tried to reach up, and Raven gave him a pointed look. He took both Darcy's hands in one of his. The bloody one he held behind his back. "Let Raven take a look. She's good at this stuff."

After a swift perusal, Raven looked at Jeremy. "I've got this, but we *should* call an ambulance."

"It's fine," Jeremy said.

"Oh really," Raven said. "And what if she decides later—"

As Raven's meaning became clear, Darcy's eyes went wide and she interrupted, "I would *never* sue Jeremy or Vine."

"Normally, I'd agree with you," Jeremy said to Raven. "But Darcy's an investor. It'd be like suing herself."

"You're the boss." Raven shook her head and blew out a breath before returning her attention to Darcy. "First, I need to clean you up a little." She flipped open the first-aid kit and rummaged through the box. "Okay, hold still."

Darcy winced as Raven patted and swiped, cleaning up blood and using a fair dose of antiseptic foam. She glanced at Jeremy, then away. He squeezed her hands.

"All right, it's clean and the cut isn't that big. The bump is gonna be a whopper, though. Already swelling." Raven pressed a piece of gauze to Darcy's head. She looked up. "Mara, you can go. Chief, hold this for a second. Don't be shy with the pressure."

He stepped to the side, using his left hand to take over for Raven. He kept his right on Darcy's and rubbed soothing little strokes with his thumb. He didn't want to think about why.

Raven dug in the first-aid kit again. "Aha! Glue."

Darcy's eyebrows rose, and she tried to turn and look at Raven. "For my head?"

"You'd prefer we find a razor and shave a spot for a Band-Aid to stick?"

Darcy said, "Glue away."

Raven spent a minute poking around. "I'm trying to get as little of your hair as possible."

Jeremy watched as Raven pressed once more with clean gauze, glued quickly, and then used both hands to keep the wound sealed as it dried. When she was satisfied, she nodded and repacked the kit.

"Use the ice—all night. Not kidding," Raven said. She moved around to Darcy's front, pulled out her phone, hit the flashlight app, and shined the light into each of Darcy's eyes. "You don't seem to be concussed. But, I'm not a doctor." Raven said, and her eyes darted to Jeremy with a sly look, "I don't think you should be alone tonight, just in case. Especially since we chose not to call EMS."

Jeremy scowled. Raven was making him worry, goddammit. Plus, she had read everything wrong if she thought forcing them together was a good idea.

"Thank you for everything," Darcy said. "I'm sure it's fine."

"I'm serious," Raven said. She looked at Jeremy. "I better get back."

"Thanks," he said. "Call me if you need me." Which meant what? He didn't know, only he wasn't letting Darcy out of his sight until he was sure she was truly okay.

7

When Raven exited Jeremy's office and shut the door behind her, Darcy chanced a peek at Jeremy. Eyebrows knitted, mouth in a hard line, yet he was still holding her hand. He'd intervened with Slimy—even though he wasn't thrilled about her presence at Vine. He found her pants hot—but had stopped her from entering his personal space when they'd been in this same room a little while ago. She was officially confused, and it had nothing to do with the bump on her head that felt like it was growing by the second.

If only she'd been laid out on his desk under different circumstances. Clearer, mutual circumstances. She pulled her hand from his and scooted toward the edge of the desk. "My car is nearby, and it's a short drive."

"I'm not sure you should drive." His eyebrows dipped —in concern or displeasure, she couldn't guess.

Even behind the walls, the music was incredibly loud, and Darcy was getting a headache. It was past time to call it a night and skedaddle. She stood, careful to make sure her feet felt solid under her. Jeremy hovered, seemingly ready to catch her if she got dizzy.

"Do you"—he cleared his throat—"have someone at home?"

She looked at him blankly.

"In case you are concussed. You know, better safe than sorry."

Right, she thought, *all that waking a person every so often*. "I have someone I can call to come over."

Jeremy's jaw clenched. Didn't he believe her?

"My housekeeper," Darcy explained. "She doesn't like to drive at night anymore, but I can pick her up on the way home."

"That seems like a lot of driving." Jeremy scrubbed a hand over his face. "You should stay here."

She raised her eyebrows.

"I mean," he said, "upstairs, at my place."

Jeremy was offering to watch over her all night? Darcy didn't know what to think, but she also sure didn't feel like a battle about getting herself home right now.

"I don't suppose it's soundproof," she said, and glanced at the wall separating them from the dance floor.

"Actually, it is."

The worry about whether this was a good idea was edged out by a nugget of hope—always hovering just beneath the surface when it came to Jeremy. Darcy shrugged. "Okay, then."

He smiled—a rare thing, and her heart turned over. Then he gently took her arm and led her into the hallway, through another door and to a stairwell. She didn't need the support, but she craved his touch, so she didn't fuss this time. He gestured that she should precede him up the stairs.

Darcy smiled. He was going to get an eyeful of her rear in the pants he found so sexy.

———

When Darcy asked if Jeremy had anything she could sleep in, he breathed a sigh of relief. Because the thought of her in those pants while in his bed? Christ. The willpower he'd been working so hard for would go up in flames.

He rummaged around and came up with a t-shirt. As soon as he handed it to her, he panicked, though. Given how tight those pants were, she probably wore a thong, or maybe—he gulped—nothing. There was no way he could lie next to her and not touch her if—

He spun back to the dresser. She'd adopted a pair of his boxers in college. That would work now, too.

Jeremy showed her the bathroom, offered up a spare toothbrush, and pulled the door shut.

He ran a hand over his hair in frustration. What the hell was the matter with him? Darcy was injured, and all he could think about was touching her. Disgusted, he shook his head.

He'd set the ice on the kitchen counter, so he went to freshen it. What else? His sheets were clean, the dishes were done, and the apartment was reasonably tidy. He chugged a glass of water, then filled one for Darcy and put it on the nightstand in the bedroom along with the ice for her head. He set that in a dish—because he knew from experience that it'd melt all over. He grabbed a couple of fresh towels.

Then he sat, elbows on knees, on the edge of the bed to wait.

When Darcy came out, his breath caught in his chest. She'd washed her face, and therefore appeared younger. And in his worn college t-shirt and boxers, they might as well have stepped back in time.

He stood and took the folded clothes she carried and placed them on the dresser. She ran a hand through her hair. She couldn't be any more comfortable than he was.

"Do you want to watch TV or something?" he asked.

"Can I just go to bed?"

"Of course." He pulled down the covers, then hovered awkwardly. If she was just a friend, this would be no big deal. He'd just walk out of the room. If she was still his lover, he'd kiss her before she climbed in. What he really wanted was to pull her into his arms and hold her. Because she was more to him than either of those things—no matter how much he wished she wasn't.

"Do you have any pain reliever?" she asked.

"Good idea."

When he'd returned from the bathroom with some ibuprofen in hand, Darcy had climbed under the covers. She looked good—too good—in his bed, and he clenched his teeth. He'd imagined it so many times—but not like this.

"Your head hurts?" he asked.

"Yes." She took the ibuprofen, set the glass of water back on the nightstand, and slid down under the covers. "But I'm getting a headache, too. Between the noise, the stress, the late night…" She shrugged one shoulder.

He nodded. "Wait," he said, and grabbed the towel.

She sat up, and he leaned over to smooth it over the

pillow. Such close proximity. He could smell her scent: citrus and mint and warmth—if warmth could smell. She lay back down, winced, and turned to her side. She reached for the bag of ice, but he grabbed it first and adjusted it behind her head.

"Thanks," she said. "For everything."

"I'll wake you in few hours."

Before his head knew what his hand was doing, he smoothed a lock of hair away from her face. She smiled, and her eyelids drifted closed.

Jeremy braced himself for a sleepless, tortured night.

———

Darcy woke to Jeremy shaking her shoulder. She blinked and tried to get her bearings. If this were a dream, he would be kissing and stroking her awake. As soon as she rolled to her back and her sore head encountered wet towel, she remembered.

"Ow." She levered onto an elbow and reached for the water glass. The last thing she wanted was to breathe yuck on Jeremy. Even the hot pants might lose their charm if he caught the bad taste in her mouth.

"How do you feel?"

She raised an eyebrow. "Tired."

"I won't keep you awake."

She wished he would—just not talking. Then she realized he looked tired, too, and he was still in his jeans and t-shirt. "Haven't you slept?"

"I had to go back down to the club, and then I was afraid I wouldn't wake up to check on you. I crash pretty hard."

She frowned. "I'll set an alarm on my phone. But I'm sure you don't need to wake me again."

"I'll be the judge of that."

She rolled her eyes. "How?"

He pursed his lips. "What's your name?"

Silly. But okay, if it made him feel better, she'd play. "Darcy Hellston."

"What day of the week is it?"

"Friday."

"Wrong."

She laughed. She had no idea what time it was. Maybe three or four a.m.? "Okay, it was Friday night late when I fell, but it's Saturday sometime in the wee hours now."

"What month?"

"September."

"What season?"

"I thought you weren't going to keep me up very long?"

He rocked his head back and forth, and then one corner of his mouth tipped up. "I guess you pass."

He took the ice bag to refill it.

"Do I have to?" she asked.

"Trust me, the more you ice it, the better off you'll be."

"Fine."

By the time he returned, she'd nearly drifted off. He sat on the edge of the bed and resituated everything. When she was ensconced in the covers on her side with a dry towel and a frigid pillow of ice, she asked, "You'll sleep now?"

He stood and turned toward the bedroom door, obviously heading for the couch in the living room. It was a big couch for a big, warehouse-style room, but she wanted him near her. She reached out and snagged his hand.

"Stay," she said. Something indecipherable crossed his face. She hadn't meant— She shook her head. "Sleep in the bed. It's not fair to be kicked out of your own bed. It's not like we're strangers."

He looked at their hands, but in the dim light, she couldn't read his expression.

He dropped her hand and walked around the bed.

"Change if you want," she said. "I won't look."

"Goodnight, Darcy," he said, but the tone was more like *go to sleep*.

He didn't pull down the covers, but Darcy felt the mattress indent slightly with his weight. She considered that a small victory.

Jeremy woke her again somewhere around six a.m. to ask her more silly questions. *Who is the sitting president? What college did you go to?* And *where did we always go in college on Thursday nights?*

He didn't get up to get more ice. Instead, he fell asleep facing her while he was trying to think of another quiz question.

He'd remained very serious tonight, but she felt they'd attained a better level of comfort with each other. It wasn't naked-in-True-Springs-level comfortable, but still…

Darcy's heart sang, and she drifted off smiling.

8

When Darcy next woke, light was streaming in around the window shades. It had to be midmorning, because she could hear the sounds of a busy Saturday in the Strip through the windows. Jeremy's soundproofing must be only between the apartment's flooring and the club below.

Jeremy was still stretched out beside her, but now he was under the covers and bare-chested. One arm was under his pillow, exposing a tuft of dark hair. The hair on his gorgeous chest led enticingly south but disappeared under the sheet. She assumed he wasn't naked, but hey, a girl could hope. He was so virile, so male, so flipping sexy that she warmed just looking at him.

The best part, however, was that his other arm crossed the small space between them and rested on her hip over the sheet. Darcy's heart leapt. She couldn't help it. She'd been aching for his touch for weeks now. And maybe this meant—subconsciously at least—that he wasn't as wedded to keeping things as professional between them as he'd led her to believe.

Add that hand on her hip to last night's overreaction to her leather pants? Darcy felt far more hopeful than she had only yesterday.

Although the urge to put her palm to the dark scruff on his face was strong, she lay still as stone so that she could look her fill. In rest, she saw more of the boy she'd loved so many years ago, yet Jeremy had matured into an even handsomer man. Straight nose, hard jaw, determined brows, and, when awake, stunning blue eyes.

Darcy wondered just how long he slept after a club shift. She lay there probably an hour, stomach rumbling with hunger, when his big hand squeezed her hip and a satisfied smile appeared on his face. She was so tempted to scoot closer, put her hand on his chest, and throw a leg over him. What would happen? Would he kiss her and pull her flush against him? Or would he push her away, angry that she'd taken advantage of the situation? What she wouldn't give for him to tug on her hip and give her a positive sign.

Instead, he opened his eyes and the smile evaporated. Her heart took a small hit at that, but she smiled and said, "Hi."

"Hi," he said, his voice rusty with sleep. He glanced toward her hip, and the delicious weight of his hand vanished. He scrubbed his face and drove his fingers through his hair before flopping onto his back.

She was reluctant to let him go. "Don't you have more questions for me?"

He rolled back onto his side and searched her face. The moments stretched on. Darcy wondered if she should tell him that other than a sore, swollen lump, she felt fine, but she didn't really want to give him an opening to kick her out. She liked being in his bed, in his home, and in his club. She'd be content nearly anywhere if Jeremy was at her side. Just seeing him a few times a week—despite barely speaking because he was avoiding her—made her feel not as lonely as usual.

He asked, "Why did you leave school?"

She hadn't expected such a loaded question, and tension shot through her body. She cleared her throat, tried to come up with words. Where did she even start? How much should she tell him?

A look of disgust crossed Jeremy's face, and he rolled away from her and swung his feet onto the floor. She noted that he wore loose lounge pants—not naked after all—even as she scrambled for the words to really tell him.

"My grades," she said hastily. "I…struggled…"

Jeremy remained sitting, elbows on knees at the edge of the bed, facing away from her. Ready to flee at any moment.

Darcy took a deep breath. "My grades were so poor that my parents wouldn't allow me to go back."

She remembered the keen sense of horror she'd felt going into finals week, when she'd calculated what she'd need to score to bring her grades up—impossible numbers. The terrible conversation with her parents that followed. The awful week she'd spent hiding her distress from Jeremy and their friends.

Jeremy looked at her over his shoulder. "Your grades were that bad at school?"

Shame rose in prickles of heat on her cheeks. She sat up, shoving a pillow upward so that she could lean back against the headboard. "By my father's standards, yes. He and all of my brothers were Ivy Leaguers. High achievers." She tucked her knees up and wrapped her arms around them. "And the fact that I couldn't excel—could barely get by—at Glenmead College?"

Jeremy was scowling.

"Don't look at me like that," she said. "I'm not my father, and you and I both know lots of people that graduated from there, had a great education, and are wildly successful."

He shook his head. "Your dad's an a—" He sat up and turned to sit with one leg up on the bed. Not facing her exactly, but close. "I wish you could have had a chat with my folks. They believe that any opportunity is only as good as the effort you put into it. College included."

She smiled. "Your parents sound like smart people. But the truth was, I really couldn't handle the work." She fiddled with the sheet. She wasn't ready to tell him why. Someday, maybe. Not now, while she still felt like they were on shaky ground.

"I wish you had told me. I could have helped."

Exactly what she'd been afraid of all those years ago. She gave him a small smile. "Thanks." He'd been smart and he worked hard—a winning combination. But even he couldn't have helped her.

"But why the hell didn't you tell me? You just friggin' disappeared," he said, and still, after all this time, she heard raw frustration and no small amount of hurt behind the words.

Tears came to her eyes. She'd been trying to save him. She wished she could have done that without hurting him.

So, this time, she decided to answer him as truthfully as she could. "Shame."

———

Waking with Darcy in his bed had been torture. Every cell in Jeremy's body ached to touch her softness, to sink into her curves, bury himself deep and never come up for air. After they'd talked about the past, he wanted nothing more than to hold and comfort her, and never let her go.

So what did he do?

In a total dickhead move, he told Darcy he had a busy morning, that he needed to shower and get moving, so she should just let herself out. She bit her lip and looked away, then climbed out of his bed, retrieved her clothes, and slipped into his bathroom.

He noted that the glue Raven had used on Darcy's head seemed to have held—no fresh blood on the towel or pillowcase. He also noted that she looked freaking amazing in his boxers and t-shirt with her cheeks pink from sleep and her hair mussed. He ached to reach for her and pull her into his arms, kiss the top of her head, her ear, her neck, lower...

Much the way he'd been dreaming about when he'd woken full-on hard for her. And it wasn't general morning wood—this was Darcy-hard—a whole 'nother level.

Jeremy headed for the living room and turned on the news. He started coffee in the kitchen and then sank onto the couch and opened his laptop.

When Darcy came out of the bedroom, she was, of course, wearing those leather pants again. He averted his eyes. He still couldn't believe he'd blown up over stupid pants.

She held the now-empty water glass he'd gotten her last night. "I'll just drop this in your kitchen and go."

"Cool." He nodded and stood. She crossed behind the couch, and he moved toward his bedroom.

He was nearly at the door when she said, "Thanks for everything."

"You're welcome." He didn't even look over his shoulder. He'd just essentially kicked her out—and yet he didn't want to actually watch her leave. Friggin' mature of him.

Two steps into the bedroom and he heard the front door open and then close.

Last night—and this morning—didn't change anything. They'd agreed to a professional relationship. That was what he wanted—for his own well-being, not to mention Vine's. He needed to keep her at arm's length. He wasn't ready to let her back in—and if he was smart, he never would be. Because what was the point? She would only put the brakes on, and he'd be left wanting.

Jeremy paused at the bed and considered going back to sleep.

He was glad he'd asked about why she'd left school. It was still fucked up, but he understood a lot better now. He wasn't sure she'd told him everything. But it didn't matter if she was hiding things from him. He couldn't allow himself to care.

He'd accepted her money. He seemed to be stuck with her visiting the club because of it. If any other dickheads got pushy while he was around, he'd intervene. And that was it.

He stared at the indent on her pillow, both sides of the

bed slept in… Empty now. Jeremy scowled, then yanked up the duvet and pulled it tight. It wasn't the fact that he hadn't had sex and still ached for it—because he could bring home somebody practically any night, given his job —it was that, as usual, he felt the loss of Darcy like a physical thing.

"Fuck sleep," Jeremy said.

He stalked into the bathroom and flipped the lever for the shower. He'd hit Allegheny Coffee & Tea Exchange for some caffeine, and then head over to his family's diner, the Wanderlust. He hadn't seen any family since he'd played ball with Jake, and this way he could gorge on a Black and Gold omelet. Best of all, he'd escape the space Darcy had invaded and score a healthy dose of distraction.

9

———

Darcy left Jeremy's heavy-hearted and starving. The only thing for it was food. Hearty, hot, and fast. Once she was full, maybe then she could think. Because this situation with Jeremy was killing her. It was like this no-man's land between what was and what could be. She needed… They needed…

She nearly growled. She'd never been able to focus if she was overly hungry. Her car was surely fine in the lot, the mid-September morning was pleasant, so where to? She thought for a moment and then headed on foot for Cafe Raymond down Penn Avenue. Five blocks or so in these heels wasn't fab, but her car was that direction anyway. She knew she must look like she was doing the walk of shame in last night's clothes. Unfortunately, there wasn't any shame in it. Just a sore spot on her head and a sorer spot in her heart.

When she pulled open the door, the amazing scent of all Cafe Raymond's from-scratch baked goods lifted her spirits. There was a line—Saturdays were not the time to get anything done fast in the popular Strip—but she was willing to wait. Good food wouldn't solve a broken heart, but it would do wonders for her equilibrium. She ordered a pastrami and egg because she'd been up half the night, it was midmorning, and she was a person who couldn't skip meals. She had a decent metabolism, and between the hot yoga, tennis, golf—well, she needed her food.

Once full, she could figure out what, if anything, there was to do about Jeremy.

Finally, food in hand, Darcy headed outside. The Strip was bustling, and she hesitated for a moment. There were a few outdoor tables, though none empty. She gestured to an empty spot at a round table and asked two older women in Pittsburgh t-shirts, "May I?"

At their assent, she sank into a chair, spread out her feast, and dug in. She closed her eyes for a few seconds, it was that good. The red onion made it, or maybe it was this particular mustard, or— Who cared?

"Heaven, right?" one of the women asked.

"Absolute heaven." Darcy smiled.

At one point, she took a huge bite. She felt a tiny tingle and looked up. Sure enough, Jeremy was winding between pedestrians on the sidewalk and coming her way. She gulped and then remembered her mouth was full. His long legs would have him next to her in seconds. She tried to chew, but as if he sensed her, too, he suddenly looked directly at her.

He didn't smile, but there was laughter in his eyes as he approached.

Her body thrummed, immediately on full alert. She stood.

"You always did like your junk food," he said, as the

stream of people he'd been walking along with shifted like minnows to swim around him.

"I grew up"—finally she managed to swallow—"in a house with carrot sticks and homemade granola bars." She scrunched up her face. "Once I discovered real food, it was all over."

He reached out as if he was going to cup her chin. Instead, he swiped a thumb near her mouth, once, then twice, and she held her breath like she was waiting for his kiss, with no thought whatsoever to all the people around them.

It was *always* like this with Jeremy.

"You have egg on your face," he said.

Proverbial and physical egg on her face. *Great*—and yet Jeremy had said it with a husky tone that made her immediately think of their time together at the Sweetwater Inn. What she wouldn't give to go back to that night and tell him *yes* to his question—instead of freezing up like she had.

"Thanks," she said. "Have you eaten? Want some?"

He shook his head and leaned close to her to snag a napkin from her spot. "I'm headed to my family's place to eat." He inclined his head in that direction. "The Wanderlust. Have you been?"

"No." Way back when, she'd been afraid of bumping into him. These days, she still wasn't sure he'd want her there.

"It's way better than this," he said.

"Better than Cafe Raymond?" she teased.

"Don't tell him." He winked. "You should try it. Carrot sticks aren't even on the menu."

She laughed. "All right then, I will." The only thing

better than Jeremy's smile would be if he'd said they should go together sometime. But she didn't care. A little while ago, he'd booted her from his apartment. Now, he'd given her a green light to feasibly run into him outside of Vine.

They stood looking at each other, and Darcy got the sense he wanted to say something, or touch her, or *something*. She knew the feeling. She wanted to walk right into his arms.

Business deal or no business deal, keeping each other at a distance just didn't feel right. They were fighting it constantly.

"I should go," he said. "Enjoy your lunch."

"This is breakfast," she said. "I plan to eat lunch, too."

He laughed.

He joined the crowd, then veered into the Allegheny Coffee & Tea Exchange. Darcy sat, feeling let down.

The woman across from her caught her eye. "You should just kiss him," she said.

Darcy's eyes widened and her heart rate picked right back up.

She *should*. She should just kiss him already.

———

By the time Darcy got home, she'd decided springing a kiss on Jeremy wasn't the right way to go. She saw only two likely outcomes to that scenario. He'd either push her away, or he'd kiss her back for all he was worth and then regret it.

As she showered, she formed a plan. A dangerous one

—to her heart. But it was the only way, and if she was going to give this a shot, it ought to be her best shot.

She would proposition Jeremy—not for sex, but for a relationship—which, of course, would certainly involve lots of great sex. She didn't know what exactly he'd been asking for that morning in True Springs—hookups? dates? exclusivity?—but maybe, just maybe, he'd considered a relationship. She felt this was the only way—to lay out all her cards, put her heart on the line, and just go for it. Yeah, there was a conflict of interest given that she'd now invested in Vine…but if he could deal with it, she could too. Honestly, it put her even more squarely in his corner. He didn't know it, of course, but she didn't give a crap about the money. She wanted Jeremy and Vine to succeed wildly. She wanted to build a career. And yes, she also very much wanted to date Jeremy.

There'd never be a good time. She wasn't going to wait.

Darcy stood in her closet, wrapped in a towel. She crossed her arms and drummed the fingers of her right hand as she debated. What did one wear when walking a tightrope of the heart? She didn't own a parachute. And it probably wasn't fair to wear the leather pants again. Besides, she'd fallen in beer sludge in them—yuck.

She blew out a breath. It wouldn't matter what she wore. This wasn't about her body or his reaction to it or the fact that sex had always been amazing between them.

But just in case… She grabbed the jeans that made her butt look best.

Only two hours after Jeremy had wiped egg from her face, she slipped through the back door of Vine. With a heady mixture of nerves and excitement, she climbed the stairs to his apartment. She tucked her hair behind her ears, straightened her shoulders, and knocked.

She breathed a sigh of relief when she heard the sounds of him coming to the door. Thankfully, she wouldn't have to wait all day to do this, nor would she have to do it at the club pre-shift tonight with the staff as witnesses.

The door swung open, and Jeremy's brows lifted. "What's up?"

"May I come in?"

He stepped back, pulling the door wide. Darcy moved far enough inside his apartment that he could shut the door. There was no foyer, just the giant living room and open but separate kitchen area, keeping true to the feel of a former warehouse.

Jeremy crossed his arms and widened his stance, obviously bracing himself for who knew what.

She knew what, though—and nerves warred for the upper hand. For a split second, she considered blurting out *never mind* and hightailing it out of there.

Instead, she raised her chin. "I can't keep doing this. The tension between us is ridiculous."

He scrubbed a hand through his hair. "I'm not mad at you, Darcy, I just don't want—"

"You do," Darcy said. "You want me. And I want you."

Jeremy went still as stone, and Darcy plowed on. "The sexual tension between us is off the charts, yet you are determined to push me away. I get it. I hurt you—twice. But not on purpose. I didn't tell you no at True Springs—"

"It was crystal clear," he said.

Darcy shook her head. "I panicked because you surprised me. I'd been thinking of our time together as a one-night ride back to the past and an alternate universe to my present. I hadn't let myself consider that it could be more." She took a deep breath. "I tend to freeze up when I'm caught off guard. And I was scared, because I always, always want more with you. I know you don't think so, because I'm the one who left school without a word. But leaving you, cutting you out of my life, nearly killed me."

Jeremy didn't say anything, and Darcy couldn't even guess at his thoughts. All she could do was try to explain —at the very least. "It took years before I'd stopped missing you. I was in my mid-twenties before I dated again. And I only tried that because I was horribly lonely. But I never let them in. They weren't you, and the minute they'd try to touch me, I couldn't—"

Jeremy's jaw clenched, and she was afraid she was losing him. She needed to get through it all. "When I saw you in True Springs, I was hesitant to let you in again, terrified to go through that loss again, but I decided that having one night with you was worth it." She realized her fists were clenched and forced them loose with a little shake. "That morning, you assumed I wasn't interested, but really I just needed a little time. To figure out if I could handle it. But then"—she lifted one tense shoulder— "when it ended that way, I decided it was just as well. I wouldn't get my heart broken again."

She gulped in air. This was it. "What I realize now is that we could have it all. This thing between us"—she waved her hand—"it's always there. And it's not just this crazy attraction. When you are near me, I feel like all is right with my world."

She looked him right in the eye, hoping he could see

how she felt, that these weren't just words. "It's possible… I think…" She shook her head. *Spit it out, Darcy.*

She raised her chin another notch and hoped he couldn't see her knees quaking under her jeans. "We could be together and stay together, even keep working together, too. Can't we? There's no real conflict of interest in terms of Vine—we've got the same goals. So, other than past mistakes—is there any reason we can't?"

Jeremy opened his mouth, but Darcy held up a hand. "Don't answer that. I know you work tonight, and I want you to sleep on it."

One more bold statement and her heart would stop acting like it was going to spring out of her chest. "I'm coming over tomorrow evening." Dear God, she might start hyperventilating. Bold confidence was not her strong suit, and she felt like a total imposter. "I'm not going to call. I'll be here at eight."

Jeremy's mouth set in a harsh line, but his gaze had warmed—or was that her wishful thinking? She turned hastily away and reached for the door handle.

She summoned one more deep breath and the last of her nerves. "I'll bring an overnight bag. When I get here" —she looked over her shoulder but held his eyes—"you can absolutely turn me away." That was fair game, given their past—or at least his perception of their past.

"Or," she said, and let all the longing she felt for him show, "you can let me in."

She hoped he knew that she really meant *let me into your heart.*

Because if he said yes, that was what it would mean.

10

———————

Jeremy stood shell-shocked, staring at the door that Darcy had just left through. His body pulsed with adrenaline and yet he didn't move a muscle. All he could think was *holy hell*. Because his brain flashed with images: the earnest expression in her eyes, her hands all over him as soon as they'd shut her door at the Sweetwater Inn, his hand on her hip earlier this morning, his sinking fear when she lay unconscious those few seconds last night—

Had that only been last night? It felt like days had passed, maybe weeks. His feelings—which he tried so hard not to have at all—were all over the road. *Christ*. He felt like he was on one of those old rides at Kennywood amusement park where you were whipped from one side of the car to the other with every new rotation of the ride.

He blew out a hard breath and put both hands in his hair as he turned away from the door. But facing his apartment brought forth more memories: Darcy in his bed smiling at him, the hurt on her face when he more or less kicked her out, her crossing his living room in those damn sexy pants. Only what? Eight hours or so in his place and he was stuck with those images?

Jeremy stalked to the kitchen for something to drink, something to cool him down, only to find her water glass still sitting next to his sink. He braced his hands on the counter and lowered his head.

Was she right? Could there be more between them? An actual relationship? Two water glasses regularly, instead of just his alone…

And if it didn't work out? Darcy claimed she'd been as devastated as he was when she left school. He only knew that it'd been brutal for him. And sleeping with her in True Springs, getting his hopes up, and then crushed, had brought it all back. Jeremy shoved away from the counter.

If she bailed again, could he handle it? Was time with Darcy—a few weeks or a few months—worth going through that again?

Jeremy turned again, picturing her at his door, laying it all on the line.

What if it didn't end? If it actually lasted? What if… the third time was the charm?

———

Darcy had thought showing up at Vine with an offer to invest had been nerve-racking. But showing up on Jeremy's doorstep Sunday evening with no idea if she was about to have her deepest desire fulfilled or obliterated? That was far, far worse.

She set her overnight bag down and pulled the lapels of her knee-length trench coat together. Wasn't it better to know now? To either deal with the hurt and pain and learn to adjust her future hopes and dreams, rather than waste time waiting and hoping? Or just maybe, to start living in her fantasy world—living her days and nights with Jeremy?

Darcy's heart beat so hard that she couldn't believe it wasn't audible through the walls. But no, she was going to have to knock.

Darcy sucked in air, sent up a swift, heartfelt plea, and forced her knuckles to rap on the door. She shut her eyes, until she heard footsteps. Jeremy paused behind the door, and she nearly passed out.

When it swung open, Jeremy stood there, unsmiling, in a wide stance and dressed in black jeans and a black button-down shirt. It wasn't tucked in and the sleeves were rolled up. She loved his big hands, would love to run her hands over the skin and dark hair of his forearms, and put her lips against his tattoo again.

Anybody else would think he was scowling. But she knew this face—she loved this face. It was just Jeremy: serious, intense, thoughtful. He wasn't one of those people who was always smiling, and unlike their time in college, nowadays he was probably rarely truly at ease. He was working like a fiend to get a new business off the ground. When they were in True Springs, he'd mentioned that he recently lost his dad—of course he didn't share much, but she remembered that they'd been close. Surely, he was grieving in his own stoic way. He was also a virile man fighting a wicked attraction to her—a woman he didn't trust, who was lately always underfoot. Who knew what other stressors he harbored?

She got it. She didn't need him to smile. But sheesh,

she sure did need him to say something. Darcy smoothed her hands down her thighs.

"So." Jeremy shoved his hands in his jeans pockets. He opened his mouth, then closed it. He rocked back on his heels and looked at the ceiling. Then he looked her in the eyes and said, "If we do this, you aren't going to bolt?"

Darcy's heart leapt—and yet she tried for outward calm. "No, I'm not. This is where I want to be. With you. For as long as you'll have me."

He stared at her, eyes still wary, still gauging. He hadn't said no yet, but he hadn't said yes, either.

"I meant every word I said yesterday. And there's more I didn't say." Darcy didn't know which words would matter to him. She could likely talk and talk, and it wouldn't matter.

But hopefully her actions added up. She'd come yesterday with this proposal. And she'd shown up again this evening as she said she would, heart on her sleeve, longing and fear tangled up in her chest.

Darcy looked down at her toes in her peekaboo leopard-patterned heels with her toes painted a shimmery pink. A happy, hopeful color, in bold, brave shoes—only eight or so inches from the threshold.

She nodded once—more for herself than him—and stepped over the lintel between the hallway and his apartment. She was still a good two feet from Jeremy, but she raised her chin and looked him in the eye. "I'm in. Committed. One hundred percent."

It took a few seconds, but then a smile slowly curved half of his mouth.

"Okay, then," he said. He reached out and snagged the

knot of her jacket's belt and pulled her further into the room—and flush against him.

———

The smile that lit Darcy's face made Jeremy want to hug her, when he'd fully intended to kiss her. He wanted to see this woman happy, cared for, joyous… Why? Damned if he knew, but it had always been like that. He honestly hadn't been sure before she'd arrived what his answer was going to be. But she'd shown up, taken that risk, and now, as she melted into him? He knew his answer had always been yes.

There was no other way. Even if it didn't work out, if —God forbid—she panicked and back-pedaled in a week, he had to give it a shot. If it worked—hell, she was practically all he'd ever wanted in a woman, so it'd be damn good. If it didn't—well, that would blow big time, but at least he'd know he'd tried.

Darcy's eyes sparkled, and she looped her arms up over his shoulders. He pressed her more tightly against him by smoothing his hands down her back. She shifted her hips, instinctually finding the way they fit together best. All thoughts of hugs and happiness fled Jeremy's mind. His gaze dropped to her mouth.

When her tongue darted out to moisten her lips, lust shot through him and he swooped down to kiss her. She arched up, her fingers diving into his hair.

She moaned into his mouth, and he went for the knot on her coat. In no time at all, it was on the floor, and she'd unbuttoned his shirt. When he felt her hands smooth down his chest and skate lower, his abdomen muscles clenched and shivers of awareness traveled over him. His hands were in her hair, and he pulled back from kissing her long enough to look at her. Already her lids were heavy, her cheeks pink, and her lips swollen. He knew how that felt—the pressure behind his fly was already intense, and they'd only just begun.

She was wearing a knit black dress that crossed in the front. And unless he was missing something, there was only one tie holding it together. As he watched, breath held in anticipation, she pulled the string. The dress fell open and she was wearing—Jesus—a bra and panty set cut in an almost athletic style that was mostly sheer except for some red trim. She shifted her shoulders, causing the dress to fall to the floor, and she—

Christ, she was so gloriously beautiful. Her contradictions always surprised him. One of the things he loved about her—so buttoned up on the surface, and yet so bold and sexy underneath. Always classy and polite, yet never shy about her sexuality.

Those panties were boy cut. Why they were called that when… Jeremy reached out, smoothing a hand along her waist, her lower back, and lower. And hell yes—a healthy portion of her luscious, firm ass wasn't covered by those skimpy bottoms.

Jeremy voiced his pleasure, squeezed her rear with both hands, and bent his mouth to her breasts. If he had his way, he'd lick her all the way down to those sexy animal-print heels.

Darcy grabbed on to his shoulders and wrapped one leg up and around him. He scooped her up and carried her directly to the bedroom.

11

The first time they made love, it had been fast and wild. Like they'd each had so much sexual tension built up that brakes didn't exist. The second time had begun with lazy strokes and tender kisses almost immediately after they'd recovered. He gave, she gave, and they made it last until they couldn't anymore. Darcy loved every iteration, every variation, every moment.

Jeremy was all tall, lean muscle, dark hair, and tattoos —pure stunning male. His touch was like heaven, his mouth the stuff of fantasy. Both of them got hot from the other's pleasure. Darcy thought she could stay right here in his bed forever. She felt so full, so right, so happy.

Eventually, he went to get them some water. She heard jazz music start up in the living room, and then she spotted a flickering glow through the doorway. He returned still buck naked, carrying a candle in one hand and managing two glasses of water in his other. He was obviously completely at ease in his skin, and with him, she was perfectly comfortable in hers.

She grinned and stretched. "I missed you."

He laughed. "While I was in the other room?"

"Yes," she said. "And before that. When we weren't together. All the time."

His expression turned serious, his blue eyes darkening. He crawled over her rather than going around the bed, and then lay prone next to her with his head propped on one hand. He threw a leg over hers, as if to keep her in place.

"What you said, about other men. You haven't done a lot of dating?" He rubbed a thumb under her breast, warm palm flat over her ribcage.

Darcy stared at the curling pattern of the tattoo that wrapped from his collarbone around his shoulder and upper arm. Some men had beasts or faces or scenes. Jeremy's ink was more of an intricate and swirling pattern that included music notes.

"I've been on dates. I haven't had a lot of sex." She bit her lip and forced herself to look up at him. The only reason she was lying next to Jeremy right now was because she'd bared her soul. A little more wouldn't hurt. "Any. I haven't had any sex."

Jeremy's expression was like granite, but his eyes smoldered. "So, plenty in college, mostly with me. Then True Springs. And tonight."

She bit her lip and nodded. That sounded lame and lonely. She hadn't been a virgin when she'd met Jeremy, but afterward? It just never felt good enough—someone touching her that wasn't him.

He tugged on her nipple, making her gasp.

"We have a lot of time to make up for," he said.

Number three was on, and Darcy's heart soared. At this rate, she'd lose count in no time.

————

Darcy was tucked up on Jeremy's couch in his t-shirt and boxers digging into some late-night takeout—barbecue from B.B. Mac's.

"This is amazing," she said, balancing the box on her lap and a gooey chicken leg in one hand.

"I knew you and your penchant for junk food would like it."

"Mmm, I do." And she'd been starving. Even though she'd eaten a light meal a couple of hours before she'd come over, she and Jeremy had worked up an appetite.

He took another big bite of a pulled pork sandwich.

"You have sauce on your face," he said, and his eyes took on a speculative gleam.

She raised an eyebrow. "Don't get any ideas. Meat and sticky sauce smeared all over my body does not sound erotic." Although, she thought, if it hadn't been for the egg on her face yesterday morning, she might not be here now.

He laughed—God, she loved the rare times when he laughed.

"Actually," he said, "I was thinking that I like you on my couch wearing my t-shirt and food on your face. But it's a far cry from that dress and sexy set underneath you arrived in."

Note to self, she thought, *the man appreciates a nice set of lingerie.* "I wasn't sure you liked it, given how fast you had me out of it."

"I wasn't the only one peeling off clothes." He pointed a fry at her. "But yeah, I liked it a lot. In fact, I'm lobbying for a replay."

"I can arrange that," she said.

He shot her a glance. "You wore much more standard stuff in True Springs."

He was fishing, apparently, but Darcy had already offered up those secrets. "I didn't know you'd be there, and I certainly wasn't expecting to be sharing my hotel room. Tonight was a whole different scenario. I wanted to present you with some extra-special wrapping."

He smiled, though he seemed to try not to.

She said, "I'm giving you an awfully big head, I think."

"More than one, actually," he said.

She laughed and threw a tater tot at him. "I walked right into that one, didn't I?"

Darcy and Jeremy did manage a few hours of sleep, but she woke first. Cracking her eyes open to the sight of Jeremy's dark head on the pillow next to hers made happiness trip through her veins and pure joy fill her heart.

She smiled and stretched a little, careful not to move enough to wake him, content to just lie and watch him sleep. She marveled in the recent—glorious—changes in her life.

She almost couldn't believe she was here. Not only was her very own career underway, she and Jeremy had agreed to be an item. They'd just spent an incredible night in each other's arms, and the promise of a rich future together shone bright. It was like some magical force was at play in the universe.

Magical, indeed. She huffed out a small breath when she remembered. That town—the one their friend Peter got married in—True Springs. There'd been a legend about the water, a natural spring that fed the town's water supply. Cold, crisp, pure, and supposedly it had special powers. If you drank it, you'd find your true love. She and Jeremy had both attended the wedding festivities, and they'd both stayed in town at the Sweetwater Inn. She hadn't taken a cup over to the fountain—and she highly doubted Jeremy had either.

But that night they'd spent together in her cozy room…he'd gotten them water that night, too. She remembered because he'd been so flipping sexy, tugging on his pants. Bare-footed and bare-chested with his ink and lean muscles both on full display, he'd snuck out with their bucket to find the ice machine. She'd thrilled because she'd been responsible for that look—his state of undress, his mussed hair, and his hurry to get back. They'd both been responsible for the thirst they'd worked up.

That night, when he returned with the ice, he said, "I saw that manager Maddie Kate shoving checkout papers under all the doors."

She laughed. "That's what you get for forgoing a shirt."

"Nope. She was very professional—didn't bat an eye." He slipped into the bathroom, and she heard ice clinking and water running.

Darcy assumed the curly-haired manager had appreciated the view, even if she had managed to hide it. "Hmm," Darcy called, "then I haven't worked hard enough yet. No love bites, no scratches."

He'd come out of the bathroom palming two glasses of water in one hand, already undoing his pants with the other. They'd slipped right off, and Darcy had sucked in air, realizing that he was ready, oh-so-deliciously ready, for more. He had handed her a water, and they both had chugged the cool liquid before he climbed onto the bed and made her body sing again.

Darcy had a hard time believing some legendary water had turned her love life around, though. She figured it had a lot more to do with the fact that she'd taken that Vine event ticket—the one Jeremy had tossed on the hotel's dresser for her when he went to get the ice—and actually used it.

After he'd dressed and left that morning—so tense and angry—leaving her stunned and frustrated, she'd showered, and then packed up in a hurry, just wanting to disappear. When she grabbed for the room key and her purse, she'd seen the ticket he'd given her and debated. Throw it in the trash, or stick it in her purse? She'd bet he'd forgotten he left it on the dresser. Or maybe he didn't care. She'd stared for a moment, and then decided what the hell.

It was so strange, though. When she picked up the ticket, it zapped her. Static electricity, maybe—except the air hadn't felt dry. She'd fingered it—just stiff cardstock— shook her head, then slipped it in her purse.

Going to Vine for that event was what really had changed her course. Being there had given her the giant light bulb of an idea to offer to invest, kick-starting a purpose she'd so desperately needed. It hadn't led her directly to dating Jeremy. But being a stakeholder had allowed her to spend time in his presence regularly, build some trust with him, simmer that sexual tension—until she'd gotten brave enough to take a chance.

So, to her mind, her actions had all brought her here,

but still, if the water had helped? She wasn't about to look a gift horse in the mouth.

She was still thinking about True Springs when Jeremy opened his eyes and smiled at her. "Mmm. I thought maybe I dreamed it," he said. "But you're still here."

She remembered having that same thought herself at the Sweetwater Inn. "You know that event ticket you gave me when we were in True Springs? Was there anything special about those?"

"What do you mean?"

"Like special printing or foil or something?"

He made a face. "No, those were the cheapest version I could order. Why?"

"Never mind." She'd nearly convinced herself that she imagined that strange zap she'd gotten, anyway.

"I saw you that night at the event," Jeremy said.

They lay facing each other, her head pillowed on her arm, and now Darcy's mouth formed a little O. She'd been very aware of him as well, but she thought she'd done a good job of staying out of his sight. "Why didn't you say hello?"

He held her gaze. "Why didn't you?"

Fair point, she thought.

Jeremy traced a finger over her bare hip and said, "After the way we left things, I was surprised you came that night. And then even more surprised when you didn't even try to talk to me."

"I just wanted to see your club, the place that made your face light up." And yes, she'd wanted to see him once more, but she hadn't been confident of her reception. "I was very impressed. There was a serious line outside, the venue is super cool, the band was awesome, the staff really good." She shifted her head on her arm. "And then there was you. It was clear how invested you were. How hard you were working, how into it you were."

"I never mentioned that the money was running out," Jeremy said.

She winced. "No. Sorry. I happened to be right behind you when you were talking to Peter about it during the wedding weekend."

"Didn't your parents tell you not to eavesdrop?"

"I tired of listening to my parents a long time ago." She smiled. "Aren't you glad?"

"Maybe."

"Maybe?" Darcy put her hand smack in the middle of his chest and shoved. "All I get is a maybe?"

He flopped to his back and grinned. "Jury's still out."

She came up on her knees and then straddled him. "Looks like I still have some work to do, then."

He laughed. "From bad manners to bribery? That's not even legal."

She rolled her hips and he groaned, his expression turning intense, the lids of his eyes dropping.

She made the motion a second time, and his hands flew to her hips.

"Sometimes, when I really want something," she murmured, "I don't play fair." From creating her own investment firm to propositioning Jeremy, that was quickly becoming a habit whenever he was involved.

"Show me," he growled.

And she did. She showed him exactly how hot he made her and exactly how much she wanted him. She even poured in a little love. *Show, don't tell,* she thought.

12

———

Monday and Tuesday, Darcy felt like she was living a dream come to daily life. She and Jeremy barely left each other's sides. They made love often, they watched a Monday night Steelers game, they ate together, and they laughed and talked throughout it all.

At one point, they hit some of Jeremy's favorite Strip District markets for ingredients. As they began to prepare dinner, Darcy asked how high to turn on the burner to boil water for pasta.

Jeremy narrowed his eyes. "How did you never learn to cook?"

"Carrot sticks, remember?"

"What about those homemade health bars?"

She screwed up her face. "Ugh. Chef made those."

He raised an eyebrow.

"I know, I know. It's certainly not the norm." Neither the menu, nor the personal chef. "Tell me about your nice, normal family."

"How about I take you to meet them?"

Even as a frisson of nerves shot into her veins, Darcy smiled. Jeremy wanted to introduce her to his family. "Do I get to eat at The Wanderlust, too?"

"My woman—all about the food," he teased, and pulled her into his arms.

"You know it. I've always wanted to eat there. People rave about it." She actually really wanted to meet his family, too. Everything Jeremy had ever said about them made her think they were good people.

"We try to gather most Sunday afternoons when it's slow. A family tradition that's even more important for my mom now that my Dad isn't with us. Jake and his wife Sadie are there anyway. I'll see when my younger brother Jonah can come over, too."

"Yikes," Darcy said, because that was a lot of people to meet at once.

"They'll love you. And Rita will be thrilled another of her sons isn't wandering through life alone." He rolled his eyes, but Darcy already knew how much he adored his mom.

He leaned over, smoothed his thumb between her knitted brows, and then kissed her forehead. "Seriously— don't worry," he said.

She smiled. "Okay."

He smiled back, and he dipped his head to her mouth. She looped her hands behind his neck, and he pressed her into the counter, bending her back a bit so he could feast on her neck and chest. With a wicked grin, he popped each button on her blouse. She grabbed fistfuls of his shirt and yanked it up over his head. She threw her head back and moaned when he took one of her nipples into his mouth and sucked hard. He lifted her up onto the counter for better access. She arched her back in compliance and wrapped her legs around him.

There was a sudden hiss as the pasta water boiled over. Jeremy swore even as he laughed.

It was a good hour before they returned to the impromptu cooking tutorial.

———

On Wednesday, Jeremy went into Vine early. Despite the fact that the doors were closed Sunday through Tuesday, owning a business was a seven-day-a-week thing. The two days of hooky he'd spent with Darcy were a rarity. Well worth it, but he was still stressing over having ignored the club.

Darcy shifted the hours she'd normally devote to working on her investment portfolios from early morning to late afternoons or evenings to better align with Jeremy's odd schedule. She said she didn't mind, claiming that as long as she got enough sleep—and, of course, ate regularly—it didn't matter a bit when she did her work. She also did some research online in the mornings at his place, claiming she could learn about local businesses and take notes anywhere.

Jeremy was glad—it meant they spent more time together because she could hang with him in his apartment and downstairs at Vine. And, of course, it was a double bonus because she'd been sleeping over, too.

Another week passed and they followed much the same routine. Except having Darcy around didn't feel at all routine. He couldn't think of any words to describe it accurately, but maybe Raven had put it best the other day when she said, "Dude, you are a much happier man these days."

They talked often about Vine, Jeremy sharing both the successes and his frustrations. Darcy listened closely to his concerns and asked a lot of questions to make sure she understood the business. She tended to wait until he'd asked her opinion, however, before contributing her ideas. He assumed she didn't want to be pushy or maybe still felt she had things to learn about operating a club.

One day, when he'd gone downstairs to get through some paperwork and then got distracted stocking for next shift, Darcy said, "You are always talking about bigger bands with more draw, but you've got a cap on capacity, right? You'd have to hit your best night every night you're open to really see that work. Doesn't seem sustainable."

Jeremy frowned. "I've been thinking the same thing. I'm considering other options, too."

"Like what?"

He shrugged. "Maybe opening on Tuesdays as well."

"Can you get enough of a crowd at the beginning of the workweek?"

"Probably not, unless it was a big headliner," Jeremy admitted. He grabbed a few bags of limes and distributed them to the bartenders' stations. "I heard a rumor that the owner that shares the wall is considering selling. I'm trying to figure if expanding into that space to gain capacity would make a difference, but with the extra capital upfront?" He grimaced.

"It'd take time, too," she said. "And a rumor hardly seems like a sure thing."

"Agreed."

Darcy hummed and tapped her fingers on her other

forearm—a move he'd seen her make more than once inside Vine as she'd looked around.

"You have ideas, don't you?" he asked.

She smiled and swiveled the barstool toward him. "I do."

"Let's hear 'em."

"I think you should open on the slow nights, but not for bands."

Jeremy frowned, not sure where she was heading—he owned a music club. Bands were key.

"Hang on," she said. "I'm not suggesting you go off brand here. But bringing in business those nights would keep your revenue stream up. I'm thinking something like sultry cabaret or lounge singers or a jazz evening."

Jeremy felt his eyes bug out—but the word jazz saved him. He loved a good jazz riff, loved watching some serious dude in a swanky hat rocking a shiny saxophone.

Darcy hopped down off the stool to face the dance floor. "Picture candlelit tables with couples or small groups willing to pay a lot more per head for a far less crowded, far more intimate experience." She turned to Jeremy, excitement shining in her eyes. "You might well tap into a new group of patrons—maybe a mature audience with plenty of expendable income, the ones who aren't coming on the weekend anyway."

Now she really had his attention. Charging more would make a difference. And they might not get a lot of the regulars to come more frequently, but attracting a new audience could be profitable. And that didn't sound like it'd require as much staffing. "I don't have tables or chairs, but…"

She shrugged. "They wholesale that stuff, right? Or

you could probably rent until you are sure it works. And the right tablecloths and lighting would make all the difference. You could even get a few antique chairs or sofas to put in the corners."

"Some wheeled carts or bases," he said, "and they'd be easy to move in or out."

"What about a Sunday acoustic brunch-type thing?" she asked.

"No kitchen, remember?" Jeremy had made that choice early on. With Vine, he didn't want to deal with an industrial kitchen or chefs or menus or kitchen staff or heavy-duty health inspections like his family did at the Wanderlust.

Darcy nodded, her fingers tapping again. "You could avoid food at some of the events if you started late enough —or just offer desserts from a local bakery. There's three or four between the Strip and downtown who'd surely love a shot to cater an event. And I think you could do something similar if you wanted to offer a meal like a brunch. There are all these up-and-coming healthy meal delivery places. Not only do they serve individual clientele, they cater events. I'm sure the extra publicity would allow them to charge a little less, therefore keeping your price per head reasonable so there's profit in it."

He came out from behind the bar to join her. Damned if he couldn't see what she envisioned. "If it were blues or something, I could ask that New Orleans-style place—"

"Moe's! Yes!"

He laughed. "You know all the best junk food places."

"It's not junk. It's just good."

"You should write their advertising campaign." Jeremy smiled.

"How about I just help you for today?"

"I like that idea," Jeremy said, and snaked an arm around her waist to pull her close. It wasn't just her ideas he liked, though, he realized, as he felt the last vestiges of a subconscious tension ease from his body. When they'd started dating, he'd still half expected that she'd up and disappear on him. But she'd been steady, and she'd shown real commitment to Vine as well.

"I'm glad." She put her hand on his chest and smiled up at him. "I'll let you know if I come up with anything else."

"You'd better. You have a knack for this stuff."

She grinned. "All that time I've spent country-clubbing is paying off. But seriously, I'm stoked that this might not only help you, but some of the other business owners down here as well."

"It means a lot to you, huh?"

"It does."

He loved to see the joy on her face. At this very moment, he'd probably agree to even a losing prospect if it gave her that look. Luckily, though, her ideas had real merit. He was already thinking of who he could approach who might be interested—both musicians and fellow Strip District business owners.

"Thank you," he said, and kissed her.

She kissed him back, sinking right into him like she always did.

A loud *ahem* sounded as Raven banged into the room. She'd taken to announcing her presence. Apparently, they were a little too sugary for her taste.

Jeremy muttered, "It's like having my mom around. A very goth, grumpy mom."

Darcy ignored him and called, "Sorry!"

Raven raised a hand in a backward wave and slipped around the bar into the back room.

Darcy turned back to him, her eyes narrowed. "I know your wheels are spinning with these new ideas already, Mr. Workaholic, but there's one more important thing."

"What's that?"

"You'd have to hire somebody."

He screwed up his face.

"You work all the time already. Even on the days the club is closed," she said.

He shrugged. "Yeah. I own a business. That's what you do."

She shook her head. "You can't work eight nights and eight days a week."

"Your math is a little off, numbers girl."

She swatted him. "Seriously, it wouldn't cost you that much, but it'd allow you to have more energy for the rest of it. Otherwise you're going to burn out."

Raven crossed behind the bar again and made a face. He made one back. Raven had harangued him about burnout now and then before Darcy ever came on the scene.

At the moment, Jeremy felt that as long as he had enough energy at the end of night to satisfy Darcy in bed, he was all good.

He eyed up her lips again.

"Think about it," she said.

He wasn't worried about burnout. It would be nice to have some time to treat Darcy to a night out now and then. And he hadn't been spending enough time with his mom.

His brothers he didn't worry about—they'd pound on his door if they needed him.

"Okay," he told Darcy, but honestly, there was no way he'd hire a manager. He couldn't imagine handing over even an ounce of control to somebody else.

He watched Darcy walk across the dance floor and then turned to survey the space. She tilted her head to one side, then the other, and those fingers continued to tap.

His jaw almost hit the floor when he realized that he didn't mind Darcy's involvement at all. Her ideas were good ones, and he knew she had his best interests at heart. Because it wasn't about the money for her. It was about helping his business do well, about helping him.

Who knew? The woman who'd been the source of his deepest wounds might now be his greatest support.

13

─────────

The following week, Darcy saw Jeremy work his charm with a band called Co Devlin. They'd gotten their start in Pittsburgh before he'd opened his place, but toured colleges frequently and were a fan favorite at festivals. According to Jeremy, their star was rising. They happened to be in town, and since Jeremy had been wanting to book them all year, he'd convinced them to stop into Vine.

Once they arrived, Darcy slipped off to help Raven. She was very much enjoying being a part of all this and was incredibly excited that Jeremy was considering her opinions and suggestions. Whether out of courtesy because she had a stake in Vine now, or simply because he trusted her, she didn't know and didn't care.

She and Raven could clearly hear Jeremy and the band talking, and Darcy was quite sure that was exactly why they were stocking bar a little early. Raven didn't want to miss a thing. When Co Devlin agreed to play at Vine,

Raven winked at Darcy and she grinned, barely managing not to squeal with glee. Jeremy remained calm and said he'd shoot them his standard contract, but she could hear the underlying excitement in his voice.

The lead singer Kirk Devlin pulled a folder out of his backpack and handed it to Jeremy, explaining that they preferred their own contract, but that it was pretty standard.

Jeremy excused himself and crossed to Darcy and Raven. "These guys have to leave in twenty," he said, "but I'd love to secure them before they walk out the door. Can you take a look at this contract while I talk with them? It's theirs, but at first glance it looks pretty standard."

Darcy frowned, unsure. She looked to Raven, but the bartender had shifted down the bar. Jeremy was definitely addressing Darcy herself.

Twenty minutes? She couldn't—

"Here." Jeremy shoved the contract at her. "Just see if anything jumps out at you."

She felt a spear of panic when she realized it was more than one page. Three, in fact. Oh *no*. But Jeremy had already turned away and was talking animatedly with the Co Devlin guys again.

Dammit. She'd have to give it a shot. "Do you have a pen?" she asked Raven.

"No, sorry. Not back here."

Darcy slid onto a stool and set the document on the bar. She read the first sentence twice. Then tried the first paragraph to see if she could glean the paragraph's overview before she doubled back to try to sort the gist of each sentence. It didn't help, and she bit her lip, willing herself to stay calm. This wasn't an exam—but there *was* a time limit, and that was a major problem. She was no good at working fast, especially if she let herself get stirred up.

The guys laughed loudly, and Raven sang along with the music Jeremy had going. Darcy frowned. She had to have quiet if there was a chance of her getting through this.

"I'll be in Jeremy's office," she told Raven.

Raven nodded, and it was all Darcy could do not to sprint across the dance floor.

She dropped into Jeremy's desk chair and rummaged in the drawers for a pad. She found a pen, but no pad. In desperation, she flipped over some papers he must have been working with. She always did better if she could make a few notes.

She flipped to pages two and three—there. Numbers. Good—she felt much more comfortable with numbers. She zeroed in on the lines. Monetary value on a sliding scale. One fee if the band played a Friday or Saturday night, another for a Thursday, and yet another for a Wednesday. Festivals were a much larger fee.

So this was a standard contract they offered to nearly everybody. Darcy would have to ask Jeremy if the fees were reasonable. She had no idea.

The other numbers on the page were dates. Fine.

Darcy looked for any bold type, any caps, or callouts of any kind, but there wasn't anything like that to focus on first. Just lots of text. Text not even separated by bullet points. She blew out a breath and flipped back to page one to start again.

Now that it was quiet, she could see that the first paragraph was very basic. Co Devlin agrees to enter agreement with blank. That would be where Vine's name, or Jeremy's, would go. And it would be valid upon signing, and for six months. That seemed rather short, but she supposed any band hoping to hit it big wouldn't want to be tied to a bunch of smaller gigs.

Darcy moved on. Paragraphs two and three were a little easier. She made a light underline with her pencil under certain words to remind herself that they were important ones. She'd perfected her own system of shorthand years ago, so she also jotted bits and pieces on the scratch paper. Almost like adding up an equation, a key word plus a key word would make a key concept. Writing it down like that kept the bigger idea—or sum—at the ready when she went back to it.

She worried about what she might be missing, because sometimes words that didn't seem that important could change the whole meaning of a thing. She shook her head and tried to think about the overall context of what she was reading. Any band would be expected to provide certain equipment, provide a quality performance, and play a certain number of sets. In turn, any establishment would need to provide adequate space, facilities, etc. She didn't get every detail, but it seemed reasonable and standard.

Darcy flipped to page two, her chest tightening at the realization. Even though page three wasn't a full page and she'd looked at the numbers, she probably wasn't even halfway. She dug her cell phone out of her pocket. How long had it been? She didn't know when she'd started, but she'd lost valuable time sitting at the bar. Tears pricked behind her eyes, but she blinked them back. With a deep breath and a mental pep talk, she started the next paragraph. She'd underlined a few more words when the door swung open. Darcy jumped, even as her hopes crashed.

"I'm so pumped." Jeremy was grinning from ear to ear. "How's it look?"

"I don't know what's normal," she said. And that much was true. She didn't have a comparison basis for this.

"But nothing jumps out at you as unreasonable, right?"

She turned the pages to face him and pointed out their fees. "Is this about what you'd expect to pay?"

"Yeah. I promised them a Saturday."

Darcy bit her lip. "Well, I guess it's probably okay, then." She used iffy words out of self-defense. She couldn't swear by it, but it was surely standard, right? And she'd tried. She really had. The parts she'd gotten through definitely made sense.

"Cool. Thanks." Jeremy pulled her to him, kissed her hard on the lips, then pulled away with a grin. "It might be worth bumping somebody else to get them in quick."

"You can do that? You didn't sign contracts with the other bands, too?"

He snagged a pen off the desk and headed for the door. "Yeah, but they get it. You sweeten the pot to get them back. Or sometimes you even just pay them anyway, and it's still worth it."

He winked and then was gone.

Darcy sank back into the chair, defeated.

For the first time since she'd started all this, she doubted. Maybe she wasn't the partner Jeremy needed. She pressed the heels of her hands into her eyes.

Then she slammed her hands on the desk. Screw that undermining herself shit. She was a damn good investment partner. And Jeremy sure didn't seem to have any complaints in the relationship department, either.

Nobody was perfect. She just needed to open her mouth and explain to him how things worked—or didn't—for her when it came to her learning disorder. And she needed to do it before he asked her to review another contract.

14

Darcy's nerves vanished the second Rita Walker's broad smile and open arms welcomed her into her restaurant.

"Jeremy hasn't told me squat about you," Rita said, and shot her eldest son a look, "so forgive me if I take matters into my own hands and ask a lot of questions."

Jeremy shook his head, but his brother—had to be one of his brothers, Darcy thought, given the similar build and features—laughed. "Mom, let her breathe first. I'm Jonah," he said, and shook her hand. "And she's just excited."

Darcy remembered that Jonah was some kind of digital artist or graphic designer. He seemed far more laid-back and easygoing than Jeremy.

"Nice to meet you," she said.

"Nice to meet *you*," Jonah said. "It's good to know Jeremy doesn't scare off *all* the ladies."

"I do just fine, twerp," Jeremy shot back. "I just can't see subjecting them all to this."

Darcy elbowed him, and he snaked an arm around her to pull her against him. "I *did* just fine," he amended. "Before this one made me forget all the others."

Rita rolled her eyes. "When you have all boys," she said, leaning toward Darcy conspiratorially, "you learn workarounds on many fronts. Like taking compliments even though you have to fish for them and, of course, taking charge of introductions." Rita beckoned for Darcy to follow her and started walking toward the kitchen. "Come meet Jake and Sadie."

Out of the corner of her eye, Darcy saw Jeremy punch his brother on the arm. They both laughed before trailing behind them. There were only two tables occupied by patrons up front near the windows, and both parties seemed to be happily downing food. Darcy's stomach growled, and she winced, hoping Rita hadn't heard. Although, unlike her own mother, who would have frowned at the unladylike behavior, she suspected Rita would probably just stick her in a booth and insist she eat.

When they entered the kitchen, a man in a white coat and black pants stood chopping vegetables at a fantastic speed.

"Sal, this is Darcy, Jeremy's girl." Jeremy's girl, huh? Darcy liked the sound of that.

Sal smiled and waved, and then, catching some unspoken question from Rita, he pointed his knife toward the first door on the far side of the kitchen.

Rita muttered, "They better not be at it again." She marched over to the first of two shut doors and rapped hard before entering.

Two butts faced them as the door swung wide—thankfully fully dressed. The couple straightened, and it appeared they'd both been bent over viewing something on a laptop.

"Hey, Mom," he began, and then immediately smiled and came into the kitchen to stretch out a hand in greeting. "You must be Darcy." And again, despite a bandana wrapped around his head, Darcy would have known him anywhere as one of Jeremy's brothers. "I'm Jake. This is my wife, Sadie."

Sadie was a pretty, dark-skinned woman with big brown eyes, gorgeous frizzy curls about chin length, a wide smile, and a black apron. Jake had mentioned that Sadie waitressed and that Jake was the grill-master extraordinaire.

"Perfect timing," Sadie said. "It's nice and slow, so we should be able to sit and visit over a meal."

"Yeah," Jake said, "but let's not waste time in case that changes." He looked at Darcy. "Do you need a menu, or do you know what you want?"

Jeremy called from the doorway of the kitchen, "Give her Dad's Italiano. It's right up her alley. Same for me."

"Hey, bro." Jake smiled, met Jeremy halfway, and the two did the male equivalent of an embrace. He told Darcy, "Hope you brought your appetite."

"I always bring an appetite," Darcy said.

"She seriously does," Jeremy said, smiling at her.

"Cool." Jake rubbed his hands together before sliding behind the grill. "Mom? Sadie? Jonah?"

The rest placed orders, Rita suggested some extras, and they all went to settle into a big table out front.

"I hear your husband taught Jake everything he knows," Darcy said to Rita. "I'm so sorry for your loss."

Jeremy didn't talk much about his grief, but he had told her numerous stories about his dad.

"Thank you, honey." Rita patted Darcy's hand. "We're all still adjusting, but Chuck definitely left a legacy. Now, tell me about yourself."

Darcy shrugged, not sure where to start, but with Rita's curiosity and immediate acceptance, she'd told half her life story before the food appeared.

As it turned out, the Italiano was a fat burger, dripping with a flavorful marinara sauce, fresh mozzarella, and just-snipped basil, open-faced on a thick, crispy garlic toast wedge. The side was roasted vegetable sticks. To Darcy, it was pure heaven.

"Before you ask," Jeremy told his mom, "Darcy and I were roommates in college. We reconnected at our friend Peter's wedding."

Darcy saw Jake slide Jeremy a look, and she wondered exactly how much Jeremy had told him. More than he'd told his mom, obviously, so *yikes*—and yet he didn't seem to be judging her.

"And what do you do for a living?" Rita asked.

Jonah shook his head and grinned, but Darcy didn't mind. In fact, she was thrilled, because finally she actually *did* do something for a living that she could talk about.

"These days I'm investing in small businesses," Darcy said. Had Jeremy mentioned she'd aided Vine? She should have gotten more scoop from him before they arrived.

"Oh, how interesting," Rita said. "Here in Pittsburgh?"

"Yes, I hope one thing will lead to another, and I can have a real impact for owners here in the Strip. Eventually, maybe some of the other urban neighborhoods."

"I hope you don't work too hard," Rita said. "Jeremy

needs somebody to drag him out of Vine and into the daylight once in a while."

"Mom," Jeremy said, "you of all people know what it's like owning a business."

"I know, I know," she said, "but I'm allowed to worry about you."

She winked at Darcy, and Darcy got the distinct impression the comment had more to do with helping along his love life than any real concern.

"Speaking of Vine," Jonah said, "I saw that you booked Co Devlin. That's awesome. I'm definitely coming."

"I'm so stoked," Jeremy said.

As he and Jonah discussed the band, though, Darcy worried some more about vetting that contract for him—just as she'd done every day since. Honestly, she wouldn't feel truly at ease with it until *after* they'd played and been paid.

Darcy asked about Rita's upcoming travel in the spring. Rita was going with her sister Reenie, and they'd be gone six weeks. "I've spent some time in some of those places," Darcy said. "I'll have to give you the names of a few of my favorite establishments."

"That'd be just great. I've got advice from loads of our customers"—Rita gestured to a wall near to covered in travel photos—"but some of it's twenty years old!"

They had about an hour around the table before both Rita and Sadie had to keep popping up to welcome customers and take orders. Then Jake excused himself to go cook, and Jeremy said, "We'd better get out of their hair."

He grabbed a bus bin, and Jonah wiped down the table.

Rita handed Darcy some fresh silverware and napkins. Good. She'd be next to useless in the kitchen, but a set table she knew backwards and forwards.

"This was divine," Darcy said. "I think I never want to eat anywhere else again." And she didn't just mean the food—she felt so at ease with the Walker family.

Rita smiled. "Well, we're all about feeding people, so you come see us anytime—with or without my son."

Darcy hugged her and hoped there'd be never-ending visits *with* Jeremy.

They exited out the back onto Smallman Street. The minute they were alone, she said, "Your family's incredible."

"They're good people. I lucked out." He kissed her, then said, "I wish my dad could've met you."

"I wish I could have met him, too," she said. "From the pictures on the walls, I'd say his sons certainly resemble him."

"Yeah, except so far nobody's sporting a mustache." He smiled.

When they reached the corner that faced St. Stanislaus Church, Darcy said, "You know, your mom's comment about you working too hard reminded me about something I've been wanting to run by you."

"Another suggestion for Vine? Because I've already reached out to two of the meal service places you recommended. They practically drooled at the idea."

Darcy clapped her hands together. "Yay," she squealed.

"You aren't surprised, are you? I told you that you had good ideas."

"Not surprised, just excited."

"Cool. Lay the new idea on me."

She slipped her arm in his. "It's more for you than Vine."

He raised his eyebrows.

Darcy knew his focus was all Vine, all the time. She reminded him that she thought he should hire somebody to take the pressure off himself, especially if Vine was going to be open more hours. "So, what if you hire Raven? Promote her to event manager or something?"

Jeremy's eyes stayed on the street ahead of them, but she saw his eyes narrow.

"She could totally handle it, right?"

"Easily," he said. "She claims she's content bartending, but she's definitely underutilized."

"And I bet she wouldn't sniff at a raise."

"I'm sure she could use the money." Jeremy pulled her tighter against him and kissed her without breaking stride. "You know, I would have said no if you'd suggested anybody but her. I'd say some thanks are in order."

"Ooh," she said, "I have ideas about that, too." She slid her hand down to squeeze his tight rear.

He laughed. "I can't wait."

15

By the end of the third week of October, Jeremy was still flying high. He'd bumped a pretty decent crowd favorite to have Co Devlin play a Saturday night. "Dude," their lead singer had said. "We'd bump us too for them." So, it was cool. And he paid them to make sure they wouldn't hesitate to play Vine again.

Jeremy thought it was worth a little extra advertising to make sure Co Devlin had a full house, but he planned to up the cover charge to compensate.

Too excited to sleep well, he woke early that Saturday morning. Darcy was still out beside him. He rolled toward her and slid his palm up the back of her leg, over her firm bottom and up under her t-shirt.

When he traveled back down, she shifted, giving him an obvious go signal.

He smiled, stroked around her bum, down her legs, and back up. Unlike when they'd had loads of roommates in college, these days, much to his delight, she slept sans panties. When he finally slid his hand between her legs, she hummed.

"Wake up and play with me, sleepyhead," he said.

She stretched, effectively pushing herself harder against his hand, then raising her rear and pushing downward again.

"Not so fast," he said. She turned over and wriggled out of her t-shirt, then pulled his head down for a soft kiss.

He smiled and kissed his way down her jaw, then her neck, before lazily taking a nipple in his mouth. She groaned, and he grinned. In fact, he couldn't keep the smile off his face.

"You look as excited as a kid on Christmas morning expecting a new gaming system or something," Darcy said.

"Co Devlin playing Vine is the adult equivalent. But you'll notice I'm not leaping out of bed."

He slid his hand back between her legs and bit her nipple for emphasis. She gasped. "My luck," she said.

"And mine," he said. Then he showed her with his hands, his mouth, and his body that he was just as happy about her presence in his life as he was about that band.

After they'd both recovered, Jeremy took a quick shower and dressed. His phone rang—odd for a Saturday morning, and not a number he recognized. He answered, sure he'd be hanging up two seconds later because it was a telemarketer—but no.

It was, Brody, one of the Co Devlin guys. He didn't beat around the bush. "We have to bail on tonight."

Jeremy clenched the phone in a death grip. "No way. You can't."

"No choice, man. The lead singer for Cyanide fell off the stage last night, and is in traction after emergency surgery," Brody said. "Their manager asked us to take their place."

Jeremy's hopes of talking them into showing plummeted. It was huge that Cyanide had been opening for the Danny Blake Band during their tour. The opportunity would be no less monumental for Co Devlin. There wasn't even anything to say.

Darcy came out of the bathroom in a towel. Jeremy scrubbed a hand over his face. "When can you get back here?"

"It's no good, man."

"Come on, give me a date—sometime in the next couple of months," Jeremy said. "I advertised. I'm gonna have to let people in for nothing tonight and pour free drinks or something because I'm not going to have anybody on that stage. I've gotta have something to tell people to make it good."

"There's no way—they only just started this tour. We're out."

"That's bullshit. We signed a contract." He looked at Darcy. She'd frozen in place, real concern showing on her face as she caught on to what had happened.

"Read the fine print, man." Brody heaved a breath, and then said, "Listen, I'm sorry, man, really, but we can't pass this up. It's exactly why we include that paragraph about what constitutes extenuating circumstances."

Brody hung up.

Jeremy swore and threw his phone on the bed.

"What happened?" Darcy asked.

"Co Devlin bailed. I gotta look at that contract."

Darcy looked as upset as he felt. He shook his head

and flew out of the bedroom, through the living room, and barreled down the stairs to his office.

He rooted around on the desk, tossing papers this way and that, and then remembered that Darcy had made him start filing the important stuff. Contracts counted as important—for exactly this reason.

He yanked open the top drawer and rifled through to find the contracts folder. Co Devlin's contract was right on top. Jeremy dropped the folder to the floor and started reading as he stood there. Yadda yadda. He flipped the page with a snap. More yadda yadda. And then—there— on page three. A whole paragraph about the fact that they couldn't be held to anything if a game-changing career opportunity appeared. They wouldn't hold any venue to payment, but they wouldn't be expected to honor a gig if not reasonable to do so.

What. The. Fuck.

Darcy hadn't thought a huge exclusionary clause was unreasonable? It hadn't occurred to her to think this could fuck Vine over six ways to Sunday?

He stalked out of the office, down the hall, and up the stairs. He banged through the door of his apartment and beelined for the bedroom. Darcy had tied up her hair and pulled on yoga pants and a sports bra. She clutched a top in her hands and looked at him with wide eyes.

He crossed the room in two strides and shoved the contract at her. "You didn't think this ballsy exclusionary clause was a little unreasonable?"

She blinked and took a step back.

He stabbed at the paper. "Page three. See? This didn't jump out at you?"

"I told you I didn't know about these things," she said.

"You don't have to know about these things. They get to decide what they can cancel over. I have zero say. None. Basically, this says they are under no obligation to me whatsoever."

"I—I didn't have enough time."

"What?" Jeremy scrunched up his face and stared hard at her.

"You didn't give me enough time!" she almost shouted, and then her volume dropped. "I didn't get all the way through."

His eye began to twitch. "You didn't read all of it?"

She shook her head, tears filling her eyes. There were morning sheet marks on her cheek. She looked like a small child.

"I'm sorry, I—"

"What the hell, Darcy? Jesus." He spun away from her. He headed directly for the front door, scooping up his keys and wallet on the way.

"Wait! Don't leave," she called, and he heard her running after him. "Let me explain."

He didn't turn around, just pulled open the door.

"Please." She grabbed his forearm. "*Please.*" Her voice broke.

He turned. "Just—"

He shook his head. It wasn't her fault. Vine was *his* business. His responsibility. One hundred percent. This fuck fest was his own damn fault and his problem—but that didn't mean he could manage a civil conversation right now.

"Stay," he told her. "I'll be back."

16

———

Darcy couldn't stay at Jeremy's place. He'd looked so angry, and she was so upset that she'd failed him. Oh, she knew she wasn't entirely to blame, but she still wanted to curl up in a ball and wail, and the only place she wanted to do that was the privacy of her own home.

By the time she drove from the Strip to Piatt Place, and pulled into her spot in the Oliver Garage, however, she was past wanting to cry. She was frustrated beyond belief and angry—at herself, at Jeremy, and at what was. She'd come to terms with the cards life had dealt her a long time ago. She'd coped; she'd managed. She knew she should count herself lucky—there were far worse things in life. She was totally healthy, plenty financially secure, and absolutely safe. She had family; she had friends. She was blessed up one side and down the other. Still—she'd just begun a new path. Had finally let herself believe she could have a real career.

This was a helluva crummy reminder that she had limi-tations.

She should have just told Jeremy a big, unequivocal no when he'd handed her that contract—and then explained later. But bringing it up out of nowhere with an audience was tough. *So dumb and short-sighted*, she thought now in hindsight. But her relationship with Jeremy had been going so well—she was sooo happy, happier than she could ever remember being. Still, the fact that she was not sharing— maybe even hiding—certain things had been eating at her subconscious.

She slammed her hands on the steering wheel. Because —dammit—the fact that she hadn't told him about her learning disorder wasn't the only explaining she needed to do. Even worse was the fact that she'd let Jeremy believe Hellston Enterprises was associated with Hellston Investments.

She'd desperately wanted this shot, and it had been accidental initially. Then she'd convinced herself that it was a non-issue because she was simply an investor. At that point, the assumption didn't hurt Jeremy in any way. If the deal went sideways because she'd missed something or chosen wrong or screwed the whole thing up, the financial blow would be nothing to her. She'd planned to absorb any repercussion, making sure he came out ahead. Her goals had been simple: provide the boost Vine needed and get her new venture rolling while gaining experience along the way.

But then she'd gone and made a play for a real, true, let's-see-if-we-can-make-this-work-long-term relationship. Unbelievably, he'd said yes. And they were now in a full-fledged monogamous, wonderful relationship.

Now her omissions seemed like a far bigger deal.

How did one just bring that up? *Oh, by the way, I*

suspect you think that the well-known Hellston Investments has sanctioned the agreement with Vine, but really, it's just little me and my newly minted LLC.

It sounded bad. So much worse than she'd expected.

She swore, then slumped back into her seat with a huge sigh.

Darcy checked the time and realized that leaving Jeremy's in such a hurry meant she was actually early for the morning class at Exhale. Most Saturdays she and Kalpani did it together, with sustenance and a gab session after, but today her friend had to work. Maybe that was just as well.

Yoga always calmed Darcy. Between the physical workout, the reminders about gratitude and awareness and intentions, and the restorative savasana at the end of a class, she'd hopefully have this mess in perspective.

She retrieved her mat from the trunk. Instead of going up to her condo, she decided she'd buy a bottle of water on the way across town and take some time to meditate while she waited for class to begin.

An hour and a half later, she did feel a little better. And if she could just eat…

Pizza. Yes, pizza was definitely in order. Pepperoni, onions, and mushrooms would be perfect. It wouldn't erase today's worries, but she sure couldn't think logically on a growling stomach. Thirty minutes later, she entered the lobby of her building with a piping-hot individual pie and a large soda.

Darcy raised her soda in a wave at Pinky, the security guard, even as she made a beeline for the elevator. But Pinky jumped up, came around the desk, and fell in step.

"Miss Hellston," she said in a whisper, and hooked a

thumb over her shoulder. "There's a *man* here waiting to see you."

Darcy peeked around Pinky's tall frame and her eyes widened even as her heart leapt. Jeremy—all in black, his tattoos peeking out of his short-sleeved shirt, his flannel bunched in one hand, looking as intense as ever—was in her lobby, standing not fifteen feet away, looking straight at her.

"If you don't want to deal with him," Pinky said, "you just keep moving, and I'll make him get lost."

"Thanks, Pinky, but it's okay." Darcy wasn't sure if Pinky was reacting to Jeremy's overall style being out of place here, the scowl on his face, or only that Darcy didn't usually have men looking for her at home, but she appreciated the offer.

Pinky raised her hands and an eyebrow for good measure. "The offer stands." She shot a warning look at Jeremy before returning to her desk.

Darcy walked toward Jeremy, her heart in her throat. He was the most amazing man she'd ever known—smart, solid, kind, hardworking, motivated, thoughtful, and so much more. He also happened to turn her on like nobody else ever had. She did not want this to be any kind of end to their relationship. She didn't think it warranted that and prayed that his being here meant that he felt the same. Hopefully, it was just a blip, a bump, a growing pain as they learned the ins and outs of being together and working alongside each other.

"Want to come up?" she asked.

He nodded once and followed her to the elevator. She pushed her security code into the keypad and then the button for the top floor and slid a glance sideways at him.

She had the penthouse. The whole floor to herself. Would he care? She certainly didn't.

"Were you waiting long?"

"A while," Jeremy said, and ran a hand over his face. "Where'd you go?"

She inclined her head to the mat hanging in its satchel over her shoulder. "Yoga."

"Oh, yeah, right." He knew her Saturday schedule, but he'd been thrown today, too.

The elevator slid open right into her penthouse, and Darcy saw Jeremy's eyebrows rise. Her place was part of Pittsburgh's overall revitalization plan. The former Lazarus department store, now the Residences at Piatt Place, was luxury living at its most impressive. Her condo was also incredibly spacious as far as city living went. As a single person, she certainly didn't need all this space, but she'd fallen in love with the walls of windows and skylights that helped with Pittsburgh's gray days. The outdoor balcony and private rooftop deck had sealed the deal.

She walked ahead to the enormous and high-end kitchen—also ridiculous, given her lack of cooking ability —and set the pizza box on the counter. She took a big sip of soda and set that down, too.

She turned toward him then peeled off to go sit in the living room. This sucked. She didn't know where to start with that damn contract. Surely, he didn't either.

She sat in the corner of the love seat and clasped her hands between her knees. He followed and sat on the other sofa perpendicular to her. Almost knee to knee—which she took as a good sign.

She opened her mouth to say something—she wasn't even sure what—but he preempted her.

"I'm sorry for yelling," he said. "I wasn't mad at you; I was just mad. At Co Devlin. At the situation. Mainly at myself."

Darcy nodded and breathed a huge sigh of relief. "Thanks for that. I'm sorry, too. I should have told you no —that I couldn't look over your contract."

"I should never have asked you to," he said. "It wasn't fair to expect you to know what you were looking at, what was standard. You even told me that, and I still didn't take the time to look at it myself."

He reached for her hands and pulled one free of her knees. He squeezed it. "I really am sorry," he said. "I won't put you in that situation again."

"Good," she said. And she was so tempted to leave it there. He'd apologized, he was touching her, he was everything she wanted, things could just go back the way they'd been…but he needed to know. She needed to tell him. "I'm sure you're wondering why I didn't read the whole thing."

His eyebrows drew together. "Yeah."

"I have dyslexia."

"So, you mix up letters?" he asked.

"That's what most people think, but no," she said. He rubbed a thumb over the back of her hand, and she took a fortifying breath. "There's loads of variation and levels in all the learning disorders. In my case, it's mainly reading fluency. I *can* read, but it takes a lot of mental energy, because for me, it's a slow and laborious process. It takes me far longer to read than—"

She shook her head. She'd almost said *than normal people*. But she was perfectly normal, despite this challenge.

He'd been frowning, but then his expression cleared,

and he sat up straight.

"That's why you left school, why you didn't pass those classes."

She nodded.

"How—" He shook his head. "Why—" He swore. "You weren't diagnosed back then?"

"No."

Jeremy gaped at her. "How in the hell did your teachers—your parents, for chrissakes—miss that?"

She heaved a sigh and sank back into the couch. "I suspect it was a little bit of a perfect storm. I was the baby of the family. My mom had her hands full, and my dad's main focus has always been work. I also went to a private school. I'm not saying the teachers passed me because my dad had paid them boatloads of money over the years; I just think there were maybe less checks and balances. A lot of times, I downright refused to read, so they must have thought I was a spoiled brat. Plus, I compensated by being highly verbal and highly auditory, so I was good at fooling people."

"You always remember every word to every song," Jeremy said.

She nodded, "I can repeat whole paragraphs verbatim if I hear them. And I was exceptionally good with numbers, so it was clear I was bright."

"So you slid by and likely your math scores carried you into college, but once you were there…" Jeremy shook his head. "Teachers at all levels are trained to uncover these types of things."

She shook her head. "I can't put it on them, truly. Learning disabilities are so complex. They come in so many different forms, have so many nuances. Even developmental testing isn't infallible." But she didn't want him to feel bad for her. She didn't want pity. "It's fine now. I took care of it."

"What do you mean?"

"I mean when I finally realized that my struggles were beyond the norm"—dammit, there was that word—"I saw a bunch of professionals, took a million tests and evaluations, got myself properly diagnosed, and started some pretty intensive therapy. Basically, I worked my tail off. Once I was more knowledgeable about what exactly happens when I try to read something, I was able to implement workarounds. Now, not only do I have strategies, I have nifty tools like a scan pen that reads aloud. I just didn't have it on me that day you asked me to read the contract."

"Holy shit, Darcy," Jeremy said. "Are you telling me that your parents had nothing to do with this, that you did all that on your own?"

By then, she'd been way past relying on her parents. She shrugged. "So what? I was an adult and not living at home anyway."

"So what?" He pulled her to standing and wrapped her in his arms. He kissed the top of her head, and then tilted her face up so that their eyes met. "You're amazing. That's what."

Truth be told, Darcy knew, it would have been a helluva lot harder if she hadn't had the financial means. Yes, she'd done the work, but she also knew how lucky she was.

"What about tonight?" she asked. "Will you be able to get another band?"

Jeremy shrugged. "I've got a couple of calls in. And

I've got a DJ on hold. One way or another, there'll be music."

"And all the people expecting to see Co Devlin?" Darcy bit her lip—she didn't want to know, and she did.

He shrugged. "Nothing to do but make it good. Free cover and skip the line tonight. And a voucher to come see a band of their choice another night."

"Ugh," Darcy said. "That's going to be a lot of free. You spent extra advertising dollars on this. And—"

"Hey—it's part of doing business. Yeah, financially it sucks, but things like this do happen." He smiled gently. "And like I said, it's on me, so I don't want you to worry about it."

"Well, your bottom line is my problem, too."

He nodded. "So it is. Maybe with all those new ideas you came up with, this won't be that big of a hit."

Jeremy was trying hard to pretend it was okay, just for her. Darcy exhaled and dropped her shoulders, but mentally she vowed to make sure the theme nights made good money. If that didn't work, she'd come up with even more ideas.

Jeremy laid his forehead against hers, then he tilted her chin up and kissed her. And, as always, Darcy's body melted. He slid his fingers into her hair, and she splayed her hands out over the muscles of his back. He dropped his mouth to nuzzle her neck, and his hands traveled, sliding all the way down to cup her rear and pull her tighter against him. She felt him hardening against her, and she laughed.

"What's so funny?"

"You—always ready. Even in the middle of a rotten day."

"Only because it's you I'm kissing," Jeremy said without pausing in his delectable nibbling. "It doesn't feel rotten right this minute."

She grinned and pushed at his chest. "Stop."

He looked into her face with a frown, but his expression cleared as soon as he saw her smiling.

"I *have* to eat." Just because she felt emotionally better, it did not mean her stomach wasn't still protesting.

"God forbid I come between you and your pizza," Jeremy said.

"Want some?" she asked.

"If there's enough." He winked. "I want you to have enough strength to continue this later."

She headed for the kitchen, opened the box, and closed her eyes to appreciate the smell. No longer piping hot, but as she took her first bite, she didn't care. It was perfection, and she couldn't help a groan of pleasure.

Jeremy laughed.

"I'm *so* hungry."

"Mind if I get a glass of water?"

She pointed him in the direction of the right cupboard.

As she started the second slice, he leaned against the island, legs spread wide, and faced her. He waved a hand at the apartment. "So, I'm guessing you have a lot more money than I realized."

She inclined her head. "I don't know what you had in your head, but yeah. I have a lot of money. Loads, in fact." She eyed him as she chewed. "Is that a problem?"

"No, but why didn't you ever tell me?"

She tilted her head side to side, considering. "In college it wasn't really my money, but my family's, and it's a weird thing to talk about. Plus, I didn't much care. I was in a new place with new friends and was thrilled to just blend in, especially given my academic struggles. Now"—she shrugged—"it's much the same. It doesn't matter to me, and I didn't think it mattered to you, so what was I going to say? 'By the way, I make money hand over fist'?"

He raised an eyebrow. "So you aren't living on some trust fund?"

She polished off that second slice—these were smaller than those in a full-size pizza, but already her body and brain hummed along better with the sustenance—and handed him one. "You know the investing I do? Well, I started with a chunk of the trust fund money, and now I manage a huge portfolio of my own. I kind of have a knack, but I treat it like a job, work on it nearly every day."

Darcy raised an eyebrow when she saw the grin on Jeremy's face. "What?"

He took a sideways bite of pizza to get the crust. "You think some of that *hand over fist* action could rub off on Vine?"

She laughed. "I started working on that the minute I walked through your door. Although"—she raised an eyebrow—"speaking of hand jobs, you haven't seen my bedroom yet."

Jeremy tossed his slice back in the box, stalked around the counter with his wolfish grin, and pulled her into his arms. "If you're tossing out comments like that, you'd better be done with your lunch."

"Oh, I am," she said, and reached around to squeeze his rear. "I'm recharged enough that I'm ready to give you the full tour."

17

———

Darcy moved around Jeremy's kitchen as comfortably as her own at this point, making a simple pasta like Jeremy had taught her. They had leftover broccoli and chicken, and he'd instructed her to cut it all up, then toss it in a pan with some garlic, oil, and sun-dried tomatoes. She combined that with the cooked pasta, stirred it all together, and…

Wow…she'd made dinner, and it was actually good. She smiled. She wasn't hopeless in the kitchen; she'd just never been taught—or bothered to learn. He'd also inadvertently taught her that cooking was definitely more pleasurable with a glass of wine in hand. It didn't matter so much if it wasn't a great success, because at least you were relaxing. She took a sip of Chianti and then grabbed two bowls from the cupboard. Jeremy should be back up from the club soon to eat with her. Afterward, he'd return to Vine for the evening, and she'd go home to her apartment.

"Hey." Jeremy came through the front door full of energy.

She smiled. He was a guy that needed an active job. If he'd had to sit and stare for hours at her double monitors like she did, he'd be out of his mind.

"Smells good," he said, and pulled her in for a kiss. "Mmm, I think it tastes good, too."

"It does," she said, grinning, "if I do say so myself." Darcy reveled in this moment: a newfound skill, hearty food and good wine, and, most of all, time spent with Jeremy. His kisses, his teasing, his company. Her world felt—God, just perfect.

"Next thing I know, you'll be baking."

"No chance," she said. "Not with Colangelo's Bakery only a few blocks away. And I saw those desserts in the case at The Wanderlust. If I want sweets, I've got options."

He peered into the pot and snagged a piece of penne. Then he grinned at her, filled their bowls, and handed her one. He had barstools in the kitchen—extras from Vine— and they perched there to eat.

"So," he said, "speaking of The Wanderlust reminds me. You've met my family. When am I going to meet yours?"

Darcy pushed around her food then put down her fork. Good feeling over. "There's a charity event mid-next week. Want to come?"

She was conflicted. Did she hope he'd say yes or no?

"Sure," Jeremy said, "but it seems like a stuffy way to meet them."

"Actually"—she sighed—"it's probably the best way. You can meet them sort of little by little through the evening rather than having them all focused on you at once. There's a lot of them. And honestly, these days it's one of the only ways we gather." She took her dish to the sink. "Otherwise I could schedule a few lunches at the club, and we could—"

"It's fine. I'd like to meet your family."

"Okay, then. Next Wednesday evening it is." This was a logical next step in their relationship, of course, but Darcy already felt a nervous energy. Jeremy would meet her dad. Most women probably worried about this. In her case, the concern was legitimate, because she still hadn't explained that her company *wasn't* affiliated with her father's company.

"You're nervous, aren't you?"

"No—"

"You are too. You know I don't give a shit if they approve of me, right?"

She rolled her eyes. "I know. And I don't care what they think either. It's like a Pavlov's dog type of reaction, I guess. My family just makes me uptight." True enough, but not the whole story, and now guilt reared its ugly head, too.

He tugged her hand. "You're always telling me that I work too hard and don't take time to relax, but you're no different. You do all these rigid, scheduled things that don't make you happy, and many of them are family related. You don't even mix in anything for fun."

"That's not true."

"Darcy," he said, "think about it. You go to your daddy's club for family dinner, a meal where they only seem to serve stress."

She crossed her arms and propped a hip against the counter.

"You go to charity events with those same club people mostly, right? You work when you aren't with me, and any time your nose is in your phone, you're reading some stock ticker or business article."

"That's fascinating stuff," she said.

He made a snoring noise. "What do you do for fun?"

She bit her lip. "I play tennis and golf."

"With she-wolves from the stories you've told me." He rose and crossed to her, depositing his bowl in the sink, too.

"You know I love my yoga."

"That's more a health and sanity check than fun, no?"

"I enjoy it. It's a different kind of fun." She scowled. "I'm not a good-time party girl anymore. I grew up, just like everyone else."

He rubbed his hands over his face. "I'm not saying you have to get shit-faced and dance naked."

Her heart skipped a beat. "Did I dance naked?"

He laughed and pulled her into his chest. "Only for me, baby," he said. "My point is you used to love to go see bands and dance your ass off. Remember you took a graffiti workshop? You said you hadn't been allowed to paint on walls and wanted to try it. And that one spring you went regularly to the dog park, just to see if you could get the dogs to chase you."

She covered her face. "I'd forgotten half that stuff."

He tugged at her hands. "When was the last time you had fun that was just for fun?"

"Hmm," she said, and slipped a hand under his t-shirt to smooth over the skin of his back. "That would have to be last night, when you jumped me in the green room downstairs. I certainly didn't let you go down on me just for my orgasmic health."

Jeremy squeezed her hips and pressed himself into her.

Amazing, she thought—dirty talk still got him hard in seconds. He'd been like that in college, but she'd assumed college boys were constantly randy.

"Okay, that *was* fun," he said, and dipped his head to lick her ear.

She squirmed and hummed.

"Don't do that humming thing," he said. "It turns me on, and I've gotta get back to work."

"But I thought you wanted me to have more fun."

His lips covered her mouth, but she sensed the I-gotta-go, later-babe in that kiss, so she sucked his bottom lip.

"Remember last night?" She slid her hands to his belt buckle and loosened it. "How your mouth made me insane?"

He kissed her harder then. She loosened his jeans and slipped her fingers inside to trace his hipbones. She kissed his neck at the same time.

He sucked in a breath. "Darcy—"

"Are you ready for some return on your investment?" she asked, and shoved his jeans and boxer briefs down in one fell swoop. His cock jutted forward, and she wrapped her hand around him.

He growled, and her attention was dragged back to his face. His eyes had already darkened and his jaw was clenched, and, much to her delight, he looked like he wanted to devour her right here in the kitchen. She took that expression as an unequivocal yes and sank to her knees.

He swore and shoved his hands into her hair.

Darcy smiled. She knew how to have fun.

18

———————

J eremy had a car, but agreed that Darcy should drive to Hillmont Country Club, as she knew the way and the roads were winding. She was a little late picking him up.

"Sorry," Darcy said. "For some reason, I didn't like anything I put on."

"You look great," he said.

"You can't even see my outfit under this coat."

"You always look great," he said, because she did.

She smiled at him, put on her blinker, and pulled away from the curb.

He asked about her afternoon. She fiddled with the radio. They talked a little about Vine. She shifted in her seat.

Darcy was definitely tense. Jeremy hadn't been nervous, but he was starting to wonder if he should be. She talked to her brothers now and then and seemed to really enjoy her nieces and nephews, but she rarely called her parents. Maybe she saw them often enough that calls weren't necessary. Maybe she just didn't speak to them when she was at his place. Maybe they had a shitty relationship.

He wasn't expecting tonight to be a blast. Regardless, he was interested to feel her family out and he was pleased to spend the evening with her. He'd figured this would be somewhat of a date night, so he sure hoped she'd relax enough so that they could enjoy it. Otherwise? He was really going to wish he was at the club. Wednesdays generally drew a decent crowd, and he knew he could count on Raven, but still…

They passed the sign for Hillmont Country Club, followed a winding driveway, and approached a large building lit from within and surrounded by manicured greenery.

"Nice," Jeremy said.

"Yes," she said as she swung her Mercedes toward the valet. "It'll be extra pretty when they add the Christmas lights."

She grabbed her purse and got out, as did Jeremy.

"Good evening, Miss Hellston," said one of the valets.

She smiled. "Hello, Maurice. How's your son adjusting to school?"

They had a brief conversation, and she let him know she'd remembered to leave the keys in the cupholder. Then she rounded the car, joined Jeremy, and asked, "Ready?"

"Yep, you?" He winked.

They hung up their jackets in the coat room. Then, as they crossed the main lobby, a voice came from behind them.

"Hi, baby."

"Hi, Daddy," Darcy said as she turned. She came up on

her toes to press a kiss to his cheek. He patted her shoulder with one big paw.

"Daddy, I'd like to introduce you to Jeremy Walker. Jeremy, this is my father."

He met Jeremy's hand halfway. "Randolph Hellston."

"Glad to meet you, sir," Jeremy said.

"You're new to Hillmont?"

Jeremy wasn't sure if he meant a new member or new to visiting, so he said, "Beautiful place."

"Indeed," Hellston said, throwing back his shoulders a notch, as if he'd had something to do with breaking ground here. Who knew? Maybe the Hellston family had been founding members.

"So," Hellston said, sliding his hands into his slacks pockets. "You're dating my daughter."

Darcy squeezed her eyes shut, putting Jeremy in the awkward position of trying not to laugh. He managed, "Yes, sir."

Darcy asked, "Where's Mom?"

"She was a bit under the weather. Asks if you could do her part at the silent auction."

"Of course," Darcy said.

Just then, a swarm of little kids ran up and circled Darcy. "Auntie Darcy," they clamored, though the littlest ones sounded more like *Dawcy*.

"My favorite rug rats!" She bent down to give kisses and tickles. And something loosened in Jeremy, too, because gone was the stiff tension that had had her back ramrod straight the moment they'd walked through the doors.

A man trailed the four kids and smiled at Darcy. "Hey, sis."

"Drew, it's good to see you."

This Hellston gave her a big hug. She rubbed his back, and Jeremy could see that her pleasure was genuine. Then she introduced them amongst the chaos of his children peppering him with "I want ice cream" and "when can we go to the putting green?" And "can't we go home now?"

This lot had to be eight and under. The youngest, Pippa, was barely past his knee, and Drew bent to scoop her up.

"Cole," the elder Hellston said, "tuck your shirt in."

Darcy said, "He's four, Dad. It's fine."

Drew shook his head. "We're on the way out anyway. Only came for dinner."

"I figured," Darcy said.

Randolph raised a hand and turned to go. Kids, even grandkids, apparently, were not his thing.

Little Cole grasped Drew's other hand, then lifted his knees. Drew swung his arm slightly, and the kid swung like a monkey on a vine. The oldest, Beatrix, had slumped in a wing chair off to the side with a decided pout.

Darcy asked her brother, "You doing all right?"

The second oldest, Liam, headed for his dad as well, plastering himself against his side.

He smiled and nodded, but his whole body belied exhaustion. "Making due."

"Call me anytime," she said. "I can help."

"I know. Thanks." He kissed her on the cheek, then turned to Jeremy. "Nice to meet you. I'd shake your hand, but..." He could barely shrug with kids plastered all over him.

Jeremy smiled. "No worries."

"C'mon, crew," Drew said. The monkey dropped to the

floor, the one he held dropped her head to his shoulder, the one pressed against him gave Darcy another hug and then headed for the door, and the one in the chair rose with slow-motion movements and shoved her hands in her pockets.

Darcy watched them go.

"He's sure got his hands full," Jeremy said, tucking her hand into his.

"More than you know," she said. And when she looked up at him, she had tears in her eyes. "He lost his wife only a few months ago."

"Oh, man," Jeremy said.

"Yeah." Darcy blew out a breath. Then she straightened. "Let's go drop some money, so we can get out of here."

Jeremy had been to a few various golf and charity events over the years, and this was much the same: a silent auction, raffle tickets for themed baskets donated largely by local businesses, some sort of fancy wine lottery. Hillmont had pulled out all the stops with a raw bar, a cheese bar, hot appetizers passed by servers, a specialty vodka station, and on and on. Generally way too much food, and they hadn't even had dinner.

Jeremy met Darcy's other brothers and their wives, a cousin, and numerous family friends—none of whom he could keep straight. He didn't have a meaningful conversation with anyone, but that was to be expected. At an event like this, people barely stood still.

He and Darcy both bought raffle tickets. He didn't want any of this stuff but put a ticket anywhere Darcy did, hoping to up her chances. However, when he saw a basket full of travel gear—noise-cancelling headphones, a leather journal, a passport wallet, a pretty scarf, and more—he dumped the rest of his tickets in. His mom would love it, given her upcoming trip, and he'd enjoy surprising her. If he won, of course.

Jeremy tried not to cringe when the sound system blasted out another horrible eighties song. For a second, he wished he was at Vine, then tried to focus on the here and now. He and Darcy spent most of their time at his apartment and his club. But he figured part of his job as Darcy's significant other was keeping her company during her stuff, wherever that happened to be. He wasn't exactly convinced she really wanted to be here at Hillmont, but whatever. He'd wanted to meet her family, and this was apparently the way to do it. He'd have to hope for other family gatherings soon, though, because he still felt he didn't know them at all.

———

By the time they'd finished the dinner course, Darcy was breathing easier, and she thought Jeremy was, too. "You seem more relaxed," she said as she pushed her plate forward.

They'd sat a little late because they'd arrived a little late. So, the other couples at their table—a few of the women she played tennis with and their husbands—were either socializing or back at the bar for aperitifs. Now that it was just the two of them, their chairs were angled toward each other.

Jeremy nodded. "It's hard to shake it off and switch gears sometimes. I always feel like I should be working."

He raised his empty wine glass. "Good food and drink helps."

"Phew," she said, "because I didn't think you wanted to be here."

"I want to be anywhere with you. I wasn't sure you really wanted to be, though. Especially since I sort of forced you to bring me along."

She frowned. "What do you mean?"

He shrugged.

She leaned forward and narrowed her eyes. "You think I'd rather have some pink-pants, daddy's-money, scratch-golfer kind of guy on my arm?" She sat up straight and leaned forward as her temperature kicked up. "What have I ever done to make you think—"

"Hold on—I didn't think anything except you seemed damn uncomfortable about coming tonight." He turned his hands up. "Seriously, you were stiff as a board when you introduced me to your dad, and you didn't relax a bit until you saw the kids."

The fight went out of her as fast as it had come. "I'm sorry. I was feeling…embarrassed and uncomfortable. Not of you—I wouldn't care if you showed up shirtless showing off your tattoos—"

"I think you'd actually enjoy that." He nudged her leg with his under the table. A little grin escaped her, and she ducked her head as her cheeks warmed. He knew full well she found his ink a total turn-on.

"Sorry," he said, "tell me what you were going to say."

It took a few seconds for her to throw off thoughts of Jeremy naked and mentally rewind.

"I wasn't sure what you'd think…about us. Me, my family, this life"—she swept an arm out toward the food and drink stations—"all this excess. It's over the top some-times, I know, but it's just…my life. My family doesn't do Sunday football or dinner together at the diner; they come out in force for charity events and golf tournaments. And occasionally overly fancy birthday parties." She sighed.

"It's just different than how I grew up," Jeremy said with an easy shrug. He reached for her hand, shifting forward on his chair so that both his thighs now enveloped hers. "It might take some time for your family to accept me, and for me to learn their ways, but they're yours. I accept them for that alone. But I look forward to getting to know them, because they are part of who made you the amazing woman you are."

That was the sweetest thing ever, and rather unlike Jeremy to string so many words together at once.

But it really made her feel like the worst piece of crud. Because in reality, the only reason she wasn't still on edge was because she'd gotten through the introduction to her father without Jeremy thanking him for investing in Vine. That would have been a debacle.

Now, if she could just keep them apart for a little while longer. She suspected her dad had already headed to the men's lounge for a cigar, and hoped he'd find a bunch of his buddies there and lose track of time.

Jeremy slipped a hand onto her knee, thumb on top, fingers sneaking just underneath her skirt behind her knee. "What do you say we head home?" he asked. "This shirt is really getting uncomfortable."

Yes, she thought, with no small amount of relief. Outwardly, though, she chuckled. "Poor man. As snazzy as you look, you're just unused to being so buttoned up." And he was, given that his daily uniform was a worn-in t-shirt with a band name or the Vine logo. "I'm happy to help you out of it."

He made a low sound in his throat and stood, pulling her up with him.

Just one more night, she promised herself, and then she'd find a way to let him know that she was his sole investor.

But she had a sinking feeling that too much time had already passed, and that any which way she handled it, the conversation would likely be disastrous.

19

———

It had taken nearly a month's worth of planning—between searching out additional furniture and decor, selecting the right group, promoting, and even personally reaching out to people they thought would enjoy the event—but Monday evening brought Vine's first ever Latin Lounge. Jeremy had known the ideas Darcy had suggested for utilizing Vine on off days made sense, and that what they'd put in place was viable. With the first night under their belts, however, the last of his reservations melted away in a wash of excitement. Overall, it had definitely been a success.

They had been wired after closing and stayed up even later than normal, discussing what worked smoothly and where they could use improvement. Consequently, they chose to sleep in and were slow to motivate on Tuesday.

Jeremy had just plated fried egg sandwiches around noon when his phone rang. He didn't recognize the number, but with all the new acts and contacts he'd made lately, he was usually glad he answered every call.

"This is Jeremy," he said. He reached for the Tabasco sauce as he listened, then froze mid-shake. The caller was a reporter from *the* most popular Pittsburgh website. He'd pitched them before in hopes of getting a feature—every so often sending an email detailing the big deal of landing this band or that to play at Vine—and never even received a response.

Darcy was upside down on her yoga mat in the living room. He spun and grabbed a pad and pen from the kitchen counter. He wrote *PittsburghHappenings reporter* and then, after another moment, added *INTERVIEW!* and shoved it under her nose.

She rolled out of the pose and grabbed the paper to read it right side up. She mouthed, *No way!* and grinned. Darcy sat down cross-legged on her mat, listening. He couldn't stand still and paced the living room throughout the conversation.

PittsburghHappenings.com was a blog and website mainly, but they filmed showcase slots regularly as well. The site always got a ton of traffic, because they kept such a thoroughly current list of music events, fairs, art shows, seasonal happenings, kid events, and more. Everybody— including him—went to the website first if they were searching for anything at all going on in and around the 'Burgh. To that end, he made sure he alerted them whenever Vine had a change to their schedule.

Good thing, too, because one of their staff had attended the Latin Lounge last night and had been impressed.

When he hung up, he turned to Darcy. "Holy shit."

"You have an interview? Film too?"

He nodded, and she squealed.

This was major. He grabbed her around the waist and

yanked her to him for a kiss. "This is your doing." She shook her head, but he didn't let her speak. "It is. They don't care about Hijinx or even Co Devlin. They were wowed by the Latin Lounge."

"That was just last night," Darcy said, eyes wide.

"Crazy, right?" He explained about the staff member. "The angle is 'small businesses that find success outside the box.'"

"Wow," Darcy said. "It was a great evening, but I'm not sure we can consider it one hundred percent successful after one go."

Jeremy agreed. But luckily, they already had a few weeks of new events lined up, including Classical Brunch Sundays, a couple of Jazz Band evenings, and a Soul Nite. This would be a perfect way to get the word out and bring in patrons that wouldn't expect this from Vine.

Free advertising was huge. PittsburghHappenings' blog would be blasted out to thousands, plus it'd be on their website. Sometimes the bigger news stations even referenced bits of their reporting—especially when there was video to use.

But the editor wanted to get that video as soon as possible, and that made Jeremy nervous. The next events debuted Sunday afternoon, Sunday evening, and Monday evening. Each event was unique, however—different acts, different vendors, different setup—and invariably the first of anything was going to have some mishaps. Plus, those were to occur just before Thanksgiving, and he worried attendance would be sparse.

"It could be a total shit show," Jeremy said. "I don't want them to see me running around like a madman."

"You never look like a madman. A very serious and intense business owner, sure, but no psychosis."

He shook his head. "I'll have to remember to smile."

"You will indeed. But don't worry about the rest of it. We've been over it, we'll go over it again—maybe we'll do a dry run with the staff?"

He nodded. "Yeah. As many times as it takes."

"And we'll call all the vendors and triple-check the orders and timing."

He paced the length of his living room, but neither the movement nor Darcy's reasonable suggestions helped. He'd only had one cup of coffee, and yet anxious adrenaline made it feel like a whole pot.

Darcy rounded the couch and halted him with a hand on his forearm.

"I promise you it will be fantastic. But you have to breathe."

He pulled in air but shook his head. "It's not that easy."

"It is with some practice."

He gave her a funny look, and pulled away. He couldn't stand still.

"Have you ever tried meditation?" she asked, pivoting with his progress.

"Sitting still is not exactly my jam."

She tugged on his arm and led him to a wide-open spot on the floor near the row of windows on the back wall.

She dropped to the floor, pretzeling her legs. "Sit," she ordered him, patting the space in front of her.

Jeremy wanted to roll his eyes and blow this off, but he knew Darcy was into it. She'd often spoken of both yoga and meditation and how peaceful or energized or focused the practices made her feel.

He sat and attempted to mimic her pose. She scrambled up and touched him lightly here and there as she gave instructions. "Sit tall, shoulders back. Shift so you are really on your sit bones."

He had sit bones? Her touch always felt good, and a better idea for releasing stress came to him. He tugged her onto his lap, but she scrambled right back up.

"Nice try, but no," she said. "I want you to give this a go."

Fine, Jeremy thought. He'd play along for now and go with plan B when it didn't work.

Darcy resumed her own seat and began to speak. "Deep breath in. And let it all out."

He copied the motion, and the exhale did feel good.

"Now," she said, "put your hands palms up on your knees like this. Shut your eyes and feel the crown of your head reaching toward the sky, your bottom connecting with the earth."

Bottom? He raised an eyebrow and peeked at her—but her eyes were shut. Last night in bed there'd been plenty of dirty talk…no bottoms or seats or rear ends.

Darcy instructed him to ground himself and draw energy from the earth around him, taking a moment to express gratefulness, and then blanking his mind but not worrying if he couldn't. Her voice was calm, and she counted softly as they breathed in and out.

The second she stopped talking and he tried to do what she'd told him, his mind darted around like a ping-pong ball. He thought about all the things that could go haywire at the new events, like not enough food or not enough attendance or no-show entertainment. Like the fact that he was overdue to see his mom. Like what in the hell he'd say during the interview.

He remembered he was supposed to be meditating when he noticed how uncomfortable sitting cross-legged on a hard surface was. Then his thoughts veered off again. Had he remembered to approve everyone's payroll? Had Raven ordered the additional kegs? What would his dad's advice be on the interview? Damn, it sucked that he could no longer talk with his dad.

"You aren't even trying to breath correctly," Darcy scolded him, making his eyes pop open.

"I got distracted and forgot about the breathing part."

"That happens. It takes a lot of practice."

"I'm not sure this is for me."

"You can't decide that after one try. It can work for anyone," Darcy said. "And seriously, you need some kind of Zen you can tap into when you get stressed."

Jeremy leaned forward and grabbed her knees. He pulled, sliding her forward along the hardwood. "I have my own stress relief right here."

She shook her head and opened her mouth, but Jeremy silenced any protest by kissing her. Then he levered up and forward to force her to recline. She kept her legs in the crossed position and stretched her arms over her head, arching up like a cat. He was a big fan of the flexibility she earned through yoga. A stream of sunlight lit her hair, making it look like the whitest gold, and he had a delicious view of her gorgeous breasts pushing at her t-shirt.

Jeremy smiled. Now that Darcy's lithe body and knowing smile was under him, he decided the hardwood floor wasn't so bad after all.

20

___

The PittsburghHappenings film crew showed up at Vine for all three events. And, miracle of all miracles, between Jeremy's prep work, Raven's watchful eye, Darcy's extra set of hands, a willing staff, and vendors intent on making a good impression—everything went incredibly smoothly. The entertainment was fantastic, the food was well received, and the patrons certainly seemed to have enjoyed themselves.

The film crew was all business, so it was hard to tell their reaction, but they assured Jeremy that they'd gotten what they needed. The piece was expected early the following week.

Jeremy was relieved to have it behind him, and he and Darcy both fell into bed exhausted after Monday evening's second Latin Lounge.

He gathered her into his arms, kissed her forehead, and said, "Thank you for your help. We rocked it." He was asleep before he heard a reply.

He'd barely recuperated before he faced a whole new

week of bands and patrons. Additionally, Thursday was Thanksgiving, and as he usually did, he helped his mom prepare extra meals at the diner, as well as a feast for the Walker clan. Darcy bailed on her own family and spent the holiday with his, except for some time she spent with her brother Drew and the kids. Friday morning, he helped Jake haul extra grub from the diner to a fresh food pantry, where any folks who had need could access it.

He and Darcy had planned to hang out at his place late afternoon, before he needed to be at Vine. Darcy showed up directly from a women's luncheon at the club, looking classy in slacks, a blouse, diamonds on her ears and wrist, and a belted coat.

It was the same jacket she'd worn the night she'd shown up with her heart on her sleeve, lingerie under her dress, and a very nervous look on her face. He wondered briefly if they had time for a quickie and then decided no. It wasn't fair to her to toss her over his shoulder like a caveman and then run down the stairs to work. Besides, he was so fried that he wasn't sure he had the energy to do it right.

They headed for the couch and talked some, but he was probably not the best company, because Darcy seemed frustrated.

"What's wrong?" he asked.

She tilted her head from side to side, almost as if she had to sort through a lot of options. That didn't bode well, he thought.

She braced her hands on her thighs. "Remember when you told me I should have more fun?"

He gave her a sideways glance.

"Well, look who's talking."

Jeremy frowned. "My work qualifies, sort of. It takes a lot of hours, that's all."

"You certainly could meet Jake at the courts for an hour or Jonah for a drink. You haven't done either in ages."

"We ramped stuff up. I need to be there." He rubbed a hand down his face. "And this was a weird week with the holiday and all."

"The point of hiring Raven was to allow you some time off," she said. "To take care of yourself. Rest and rejuvenate."

"Things are going really well right now. This was the goal." Did he really need to remind her of that?

Darcy heaved out a breath. "I get that. You know I do. But you're working so hard and wound so tight about it all that you aren't even enjoying it. Plus, you and I"—she waved her hand between them—"we don't even have time to chill together, let alone talk and…"

Something crossed her face that he didn't have the energy to decipher, but she mumbled, "There's just things we should be talking about."

Frustrated, he stood and faced her, his jaw tight. "I can't afford to take time off, Darcy. Vine isn't going to run itself, and right now is the worst time to slack off."

She threw up her hands. "I'm not saying you should shirk your duties or play hooky for a whole day. But you can take some time to smell the roses and take care of yourself and be with me. And meditation really would do wonders for your stress level."

Meditation again. He shook his head, and a smile nudged its way onto his face despite his annoyance. Darcy was full of intriguing contradictions. Diamonds, an e-note-book, and spot-on business suggestions one day; yoga pants and oms the next; energetic and vocal bed play; and messy, high-calorie food somewhere in between.

He bet if he suggested they run over to Cafe Raymond or Colangelo's, she'd forget all about trying to lower his stress level. The thought made him chuckle.

She scowled.

"I'm not laughing at you or your meditation," he said. "And I know we need some good quality time together. I'm sorry."

She threw up her hands as she stood. "We haven't even celebrated your interview."

"We'll celebrate the day it airs—Tuesday. Vine is closed, so it's perfect." He turned his palms up. "I won't cook; we'll order dinner and open a nice bottle of wine or champagne. We'll watch the video, read the article, and then just hang out in a lazy, restful celebration, okay?"

Darcy nodded, but she rubbed the stress point on her forehead between her eyebrows.

"Come here," he said, and returned to the couch, pulling her with him. She heaved a sigh as if she were defeated, then sat beside him and dropped her head on his shoulder.

"How was the luncheon?" He stroked her hair, marveling, as always, at the silky texture.

She told him about her day, and after some time, he finally felt her relax.

Jeremy, however, didn't. His mind was full of looming tasks and employees and vendors and more. Darcy had a point about spending quality time with him. Because work was absolutely where his head was, and so most of their conversation centered on that, too. And that was…not great. She needed a date, probably, some attention focused just on her.

Hell, he guessed he probably needed that kind of break too. Here he was, with Darcy tucked up against him, and all he could think about was work. She was right. Something had to give.

Suddenly, he tensed as a terrible suspicion crossed his mind—was she frustrated enough that she might leave him? Walk away again?

Before Jeremy knew it, Tuesday afternoon had arrived. He had only a couple of hours before Darcy arrived to celebrate the PittsburghHappenings article's release with him.

He collapsed on the bed, all in for a serious nap. Unfortunately, sleep wouldn't come. He couldn't turn his brain off, and his body felt like it was wired with electricity. Jeremy punched the pillow and rose. Apparently, he hadn't relaxed in so long that his body didn't actually remember how.

He'd grown up in a family that owned a small but demanding business. He'd seen his parents harried plenty of times, and certainly running the diner took a lot of hours. But he didn't recall either of them in a constant state of stress. Was it because there were two of them? Unlikely. Along with the business, they'd had three boys to contend with.

Jeremy went to the bathroom and splashed some cold water on his face. He popped open a seltzer in the kitchen. Poked through the fridge even though he wasn't hungry. Picked up a pile of mail and then tossed it aside. He was still thinking about his parents and decided to ring his mom.

"We're all set for tomorrow," Rita Walker said nearly right off. She assumed—go figure—that he was calling about Vine. He'd made plans to throw a small gathering for the staff in order to thank them for their excellent work on the new events.

"You think we need another couple of appetizers?"

"I think your order is perfect," she said, "but maybe if you want extras for the staff to take home?"

"Nah, you're right," he said, before switching to his real agenda. "Hey, Mom, did you and dad ever feel like you couldn't escape from the stress of running Wanderlust?"

"At times," she said. "But we tried hard to keep a balance for you kids."

"Like how?"

"Well," she said, "we just made sure to have a life outside the restaurant. Made sure we had good staff in place so that we could still gather with our neighbors and friends for barbecues and host birthday parties and end-of-season potlucks or whatever. We took turns so we could attend all the games and school events you kids had." She paused, obviously thinking. "We always had our Pirates tickets, which was essentially our date night. Oh, and for years we did that bowling league, remember?"

"I'd forgotten that," Jeremy said. "Dad scored a perfect game once, didn't he?"

She chuckled. "Just once, but he crowed about it forever."

Jeremy ran his hand through his hair. Bowling probably wasn't going to work for him.

"You stressed, hon?" Rita asked, and he heard real concern in her voice.

"Yeah. Darcy's pushing me to take some time off."

"Like a vacation?"

The thought popped in his head that he should whisk her away to True Springs so they could redo that magical night without the sucky ending, but he shook it off. Vine was busy. Two or three nights away would freak him out. "Nah, just, like, step back a little."

"Darcy is obviously a smart woman," Rita said. "You do need to take some time to relax."

"Yeah, well, I'm not sure I remember how."

"It's not something you forget, it's just something you neglect." She seemed to cover the phone for a moment as she gave someone an order. Jeremy shook his head. He'd called the queen of multitasking to ask how to relax.

"Sorry, hon," Rita said. "Listen, you just have to take a little time to do things you enjoy. Join a basketball league again, or put your earphones on and go work out. Take Darcy to see a band or stroll along the river. Just don't talk or think about work while you're doing any of it."

"And there's the rub," he said.

"Yep," she said. Then "No, not that table—" He heard her curse mildly under her breath. "Hon, I gotta go. We're training someone new, and, well, you know."

"I do, Mom. Thanks. See you tomorrow."

Jeremy hung up the phone, shaking his head. Had he gotten answers? Yes and no.

He definitely needed to take Darcy out for some kind of date. As for him? Maybe not a league, but yeah, he could make sure he and Jake met regularly to shoot hoops.

He could likely drag Jonah in, too. There wasn't much time to talk business when you were panting and cussing.

But what about the odd times like this—when he found himself alone and couldn't even turn it off long enough to take a power nap? Maybe it was like Darcy's meditation, and it just took practice.

He went back in to lie down. But rather than sleeping, he found himself staring at the ceiling and getting tenser and tenser.

Was Vine worth barely enjoying life? He'd never intended to own it forever, like his parents had owned The Wanderlust, but it was still in its early stages.

He blew out a breath, sat up, and swung his legs over the edge of the bed. Had he not realized how much work it would be? No—he'd had a pretty good idea. Why, then, had he followed this path?

He'd wanted a job or a business that jazzed him—and music and bands always had. Since he was a teenager, there was nothing he enjoyed more than going out to see a new band or an old favorite. He soaked in the music as if he needed it to breathe.

He sat up straight as it dawned on him. Back then, even at home, he was always listening to music. He played album after album on the turntable. Sometimes doing homework or chores, many times just sacked out on the couch, feet propped on the coffee table, with his eyes shut.

Just chilling. Just listening. With no agenda except pleasure. No ear toward whether an artist or band was good enough for the club. No thoughts of whether they'd draw crowds.

He wasn't a stop-and-smell-the-roses kind of guy, and

he had a hard time picturing himself successfully meditating, but he sure as hell could listen to music.

Jeremy jumped up. He'd been so busy with Vine that he'd never unpacked all his boxes when the building was done. Instead, he'd shoved everything into a storage space behind his laundry room. How fast, he wondered, could he find the boxes that held his album collection and turntable?

21

When Darcy arrived at Jeremy's with a nice bottle of wine in hand, she found him sprawled out on the couch: head back, legs spread, arms and hands upturned and relaxed—practically a yoga pose.

Music—maybe Muddy Waters, she thought—blared, and she realized he'd set up a turntable. This was an actual record. There were boxes strewn in the far corner and numerous stacks of albums on the floor, plus another, smaller stack on the coffee table in front of him.

She shut the door quietly behind her in case he was asleep and then shook her head. The music was loud enough that the door closing wouldn't wake him. Still, she couldn't help tiptoeing across the room.

He opened his eyes and a smile spread across his face. It was astounding—not a forced smile or distracted stretch of the mouth but a genuine, easy smile. She smiled in return—joy begetting joy.

"Hey, babe," he said. "Look what I found."

She gestured to the room. "I see."

He shook his head lazily against the couch cushions. "Uh-uh. I found my own way of meditating."

"Of course." Darcy put her hand to her forehead and grinned. "Music is your Zen."

"Music is my Zen," he repeated, then patted the seat next to him. "Come and listen with me."

Darcy and Jeremy listened to music for about an hour. He hopped up now and then to switch albums or songs. He talked—told her what he loved about Muddy Waters, what he found so magical about a particular Van Morrison song, how he'd come to love jazz and more. At times, though, they'd just sit quietly and listen.

Darcy marveled at the change in him. She hadn't seen him this relaxed since…probably college.

Soon enough, her stomach growled audibly, and they placed the takeout order. She uncorked the wine and grabbed some pretzels to tide her over.

As soon as the food came, he dished it out and she poured drinks. They carried everything to the living room, and Jeremy turned off the music. It felt oddly silent after all those good vibes, but neither of them wanted to miss a word of the PittsburghHappenings piece. Jeremy set up his laptop on the coffee table and clicked through to the website.

"Let's toast," she said, and handed him a glass. "To a packed house and much success."

They clinked glasses, sipped the crisp white, and then, with a sparkle in his eye, he leaned over and kissed her, almost making her forget there was an agenda.

He asked, "Article first or video?"

"Video," she said. She was dying to see what they'd captured from the new events they'd instituted.

He popped a veggie spring roll in his mouth, wiped his hands on his napkin, and hit play. She dug into her pad thai.

Darcy could see how stoked Jeremy was, and she was so pleased. She felt happy and excited and…well, proud. Because yes, she'd helped Vine financially, but her ideas for growing his business had really been the catalyst for this interview. And between the write-up and the video, surely great things would follow.

The video was good. They caught some of the performances, but they also included shots Darcy thought were just as important: the attendees looking like they were thoroughly enjoying themselves, the staff working efficiently, the ambiance they'd created. All of it was interspersed with little snippets of Jeremy's interview. The reviewer's questions were spot-on, allowing Jeremy to explain that Vine was still showcasing popular bands on weekends but wanted to bring something more to the community as well, and that he was enjoying the chance to collaborate with more artists and other small business owners in the area.

"It's perfect," Darcy said at the end. She'd been so entranced that she'd barely touched her food. "Shorter than I thought, though."

"They keep this stuff pretty tight," he said. "Nobody stays tuned in long enough to go in depth."

"Are you pleased?"

"Hell yes."

She scooted forward and reached for a spring roll. "Now the interview."

It was challenging for them both to read at once on the small screen with plates on their laps, so Jeremy took over reading aloud. The reporting began like a typical article, introducing Vine as an up-and-coming club in the Pittsburgh area, located in the hip Strip District.

"Blah blah blah," he said.

"Don't," she said. "Read me every word."

He chuckled. "I just want to see what else they said, and then I'll focus on the details."

He set his plate aside, skimmed some more, and then made a sound of disgust.

"What's wrong?" she asked.

He made a face. "It describes me as a 'dark pirate who's piercing intensity alone should float this venture.'"

She laughed. "So?"

He shook his head. "You would think enough people had body art these days that they wouldn't associate ink with pirates."

"It's not just the tattoos," she said. He'd worn a black button-down with the sleeves rolled up, and the tattoo on his right arm had definitely been visible. His dark coloring and intense expression certainly had something to do with it, and he'd been sporting a couple-day shadow, too. She reached out and ran her hand over his scruff. "I love…the description."

She almost blurted, *I love you,* but refrained. Neither of them had said those words yet, but there was no doubt. She probably always had loved him. And she believed he felt the same.

Jeremy read some more, then said, "Excellent—they put it in."

"What?"

"I never got a chance to thank your father in person.

So, I figured it'd be cool to mention it in the interview. You know, build some goodwill for Hellston."

Darcy's stomach dropped out at his words, and the noodles in her mouth suddenly felt like worms.

"Here," he said, and turned the screen toward her.

Darcy fought a gag and blinked a couple of times before she could focus where his finger pointed. He read aloud, "'I'd like to thank Darcy and Randolph Hellston for believing in Vine. It's heartening to see a big investment firm take an interest in small, local business.'"

Jeremy turned to her, grinning, so pleased. Her eyes welled. She feared the mouthful of food she couldn't swallow might erupt.

He squeezed her hand, and she squeezed back as if it might be the last time she could. He probably thought the tears meant she was overcome with emotion. Oh, she was overcome, all right…

He read a line or two more then flopped back on the couch with a satisfied grin.

She managed to spit the noodles in her napkin. She set her plate on the table and turned to him. "So, you need to know—"

His cell phone rang then, and since it was right there on the table, they could both see that it announced his mom.

"Hang on," he said.

Rita had just seen the piece and was so excited that Darcy could hear every word. She took her plate to the kitchen and tried to stay calm. Despite the fact that her stomach was suddenly roiling with greasy food, this was only a misunderstanding, right? She'd never ever actually said that her dad was involved. Absolutely her bad for not spelling that out in the first place, but…Jeremy wouldn't freak, would he?

Panic rose. He might not have freaked long ago, but now it was in print. For all the world to see and believe, too.

Oh God, what had she been thinking not telling him sooner? She'd tried, honestly. But every time she had gotten her nerve up, it'd quickly become clear that his head was consumed with work and he wasn't interested in any serious conversation. Terrified of rocking the boat when she'd finally had her life on track, she'd backed off, making a play instead for them to spend more time together. Because if they'd had more time, she would have had better opportunity to broach the subject when he was more receptive, right?

No—she was the biggest, most naive, most unbelievably stupid idiot for trying to buy herself time… She shouldn't have let anything stop her. She should have stamped her foot and demanded his attention and shouted the truth.

The phone rang again—Jonah. Immediately after came Raven's call. Jake had also tried, so Jeremy called him back. Jeremy walked as he talked, circling through the large space of the living room, carrying his dish to the sink, eating the last spring roll and bringing in the empty container. He leaned in and kissed Darcy while he listened to his brother.

His Aunt Reenie called, and then a cousin, and then an old friend.

Darcy grew more and more consumed with dread. She smelled smoke and wondered if she was losing it.

Then, out of nowhere, sirens blared so loud that they

both crossed to the windows. Firetrucks had roared onto the street and converged practically right below them.

"Shit," he told whoever was now on the phone, "I gotta go." He shoved open the window, and they both stuck their heads out as firefighters hopped off the truck and scrambled toward flames.

It wasn't Jeremy's building. Darcy thought it was two doors down. But this neighborhood was jammed cheek to jowl, and not all of the buildings had been renovated like his. With old wiring and old wood and close proximity…

Darcy's bad feeling grew exponentially.

22

Jeremy could not have been more grateful for the firefighters' quick response and hard work. Several chaotic, stressful hours had passed, but his neighbor's place wasn't a total loss, none of the surrounding buildings had caught fire, and Vine had escaped with only a little water damage. The runoff from all the hoses had seeped under the door and flowed down the front hallway. Because that had happened once before from an insane rain that caused flash flooding, Vine now owned sandbags, and Jeremy had had the good sense to go in and block off what he could before it got too bad.

Still, a little water made a huge mess, and he and Darcy worked late into the night on cleanup. He manned the wet-vac, and she'd made numerous trips back and forth to the washer and dryer with all the zillions of towels they'd soaked. He certainly couldn't wait for Vine's linen service in this case.

They'd be opening Wednesday night as scheduled, and

he was determined to hold the small staff party before opening, as planned.

The flooring was industrial grade—thankfully. He thought the baseboards were probably fine, but he made a mental note to have a mold service do an assessment in case water seeped under the walls.

It'd be a terrible time to close for repairs—he was hoping for an even better turnout after the video and article —but that aspect would be out of his control.

By the time they were through, he and Darcy were sweaty, grungy, and exhausted. She, in particular, looked dead on her feet. He was used to being up half the night owning Vine, but she still wasn't, he supposed.

"You go first," he told her as he turned the shower on.

She nodded. They both made quick work of getting clean and fell into bed tired to their bones.

"Thanks," he said as he pulled her in to spoon with him.

"I'd do anything for you," she said, her voice already raspy with sleep. "Always. You have to remember that."

Both Jeremy and Darcy had obligations early Wednesday, and they kept them, since there was nothing more they could do for Vine but let it dry out.

Two hours before opening, they tucked away fans and set the club to rights. Rita and Jake arrived with platters of munchies and sandwiches. Darcy helped his mom get everything set up on the bar, while Jeremy caught up with Jake. He opened a few bottles of champagne, and Jake poured it into plastic cups—since Vine didn't own champagne flutes.

Raven arrived and asked what she could do.

"Just enjoy," Jeremy told her, and handed her a cup of champagne.

Raven grinned. "Fancy."

He laughed and passed out more as he greeted his staff one by one.

When everyone had been accounted for, Jeremy raised his own cup. "To the best staff. Whether we're doing the usual"—he gestured to the bar—"or trying something new, I'm damn lucky to have you with me. Thanks to each and every one of you."

Shouts went up, and one troublemaker hollered, "Bonuses?"

Jeremy laughed. "Working on it." He stole a glance at Darcy, and she smiled. They'd actually talked about the eventual possibility of giving his full-timers more of a stake in seeing Vine thrive. It was a ways off, though.

Just then, he heard the door bang open in front, and he frowned. Everybody turned, surprised at the loud noise. Probably thinking the same thing he was: wasn't everybody already here?

Footsteps echoed down the long hallway, and then a tall, gray-haired man came into view. His nostrils flared when he saw the scene before him. It took Jeremy a second to place him, but it was—

"Daddy?" Darcy said.

———

Darcy's half-forced celebratory mood vanished into swamping dread the second she laid eyes on her father. "What are you doing here?"

"What am I doing here?" Randolph Hellston wasn't even yelling, but his angry voice felt thunderous regardless. He was a man used to making himself heard, this was a space built for excellent acoustics, and the small crowd had gone dead quiet—a bad combination.

"I want to know why Walker here"—he flung a hand toward Jeremy—"thinks I've condoned supporting some nightclub." His mouth twisted as his hand flipped upward in a question that seemed to include the four walls and ceilings of Vine.

Jeremy was about six feet away on her left. From the corner of her eye, she saw him turn toward her. He moved like a statue—stiff as stone, and in slow motion, like someone was pushing him against his will.

Darcy wanted to crumple at his feet and blubber, but she raised her chin, straightened her shoulders, and turned so that she faced both her father and Jeremy. Just seeing her father reminded her she was a Hellston. She might be a complete idiot, but she had standards and she had her pride.

"I started my own investment firm. It's called Hellston Enterprises. Not"—she directed this at Jeremy, whose expression was terrifying in its blankness—"Hellston Investments." She turned back to include both men— trying her damnedest to ignore the many other faces of Jeremy's family and friends—and said, "Jeremy thought —" She shook her head. "I *let* him think that my company was part of Hellston Investments."

"Darcy," her father said. "That is..." So much in those

unsaid words: disbelief, disappointment, incredulity, and even a hearty measure of scolding. He shook his head, probably deciding better about expressing his personal disappointment in her amongst outsiders. "Now I'm going to have every Tom, Dick, and Harry knocking on my firm's door looking for handouts."

She couldn't care less about ramifications for her father. His secretary wouldn't let any Tom, Dick, or Harry in the door anyway.

She stepped toward Jeremy. "I intended to tell you—"

But he sidestepped and approached her father. He told him, "I'll ask PittsburghHappenings to make a correction."

Then he spun, barreling past her without even looking at her. Before she could blink, he'd crossed the dance floor and through the private door to the back. Had he gone to his office, up to his apartment, or out to the street?

She took two steps to follow him, but Jake put his hand on her arm.

"He needs a little time to cool down first," Jake said. "Always has." She wasn't sure what Jake's eyes held—sympathy, empathy, pity? But it didn't matter—she only cared what Jeremy was thinking.

She took a deep breath and nodded.

From behind her, Rita clapped her hands. "Okay, folks. You've got a club to open soon, so eat up. I refuse to take any of this food back to the Wanderlust with me."

People moved; people talked. Once Darcy felt like all eyes weren't lasered on her, she was able to turn around. Rita had approached her father, and Darcy heard her ask if he'd like a bite to eat from the Strip's very best diner. Darcy forced herself to approach them rather than slinking out the door.

"Thank you," she told Rita, nodding at the staff converging at the bar and filling plates. She didn't trust her voice with too many words. To her father, she said, "I'll come to your office tomorrow."

She brushed past her father and walked down the long hallway to the front door and outside to the street. She owed Jeremy an explanation and the biggest apology of all, but Jake's advice was sound, even though it sucked. She had to escape and kill just a little time. Then she was going to find Jeremy—whether he'd cooled down or not.

23

———————

The second Darcy entered Jeremy's apartment, he rounded on her, anger crystal clear in his loud voice and rapid-fire words. "Why—why the hell would you do it? Why not just tell me in the first place that you were solo?"

"I intended to!" Darcy's emotions were running high, too. "But I panicked and didn't get it explained right away. And then…I…I was scared that it would ruin everything."

He shook his head and tossed up his hands.

Yes, she agreed. Obviously, she *had* ruined everything —and in spectacular fashion.

"Investing in Vine meant everything to me," she said, desperate to explain but not sure how. "It was bigger than you. Every hope and dream I ever had, everything I've always wanted to change about my life was—is—tied up in this."

Jeremy looked skeptical. Disgusted. Furious. He turned his back, and she sensed that he was shutting down, that in no time he'd be blocking her out permanently.

She couldn't let him do that. "I didn't think you'd understand. You've always worked. You've always had something to be proud of. I had none of that. Did you know I've never had a job until now?"

He gave a harsh laugh. "Whatever."

"It's true," she said.

"Not like you had to work."

"That's part of it, yes," she admitted. "And in my family, any of the jobs I might have managed were forbidden. They were beneath a Hellston."

How to explain? She took a breath and stepped around to make him face her. "When my father made me leave school, he marked me as a failure. He didn't ever encourage me to go back. I didn't have a college degree until two years ago. I finally got it online, because I thought it would make me feel better. It didn't. I didn't know the first thing about how to start a career. I still don't."

"Bullshit. You do all that investing."

"But it's just for me. And it's just money. Dollars that do nothing but grow." Her voice cracked. It might have been enough for some people, but it wasn't enough for her. "It doesn't involve other people. Hardly anyone even knows I do it."

"Why didn't you just go and work for Daddy Warbucks?" He shot out a hand toward the floor as if her father was still standing in the club below.

"You still don't understand." Tears filled her eyes. It still hurt. It would always hurt. And she'd never told anyone, but she had to be honest now if she had any chance of keeping Jeremy. "He wouldn't hear of it. He didn't want me. My own father didn't want me associated with his company."

———

Even through his hurt and anger, Jeremy's heart twisted with pain for Darcy. Yet he forced any sympathy away. He didn't have room for more of her bullshit. Because it seemed they were constantly replaying this issue. He turned—he had to get out of here. Who cared that it was his apartment? It was more expedient to go than to make her leave.

She grabbed his arm. "I don't expect you to understand, I really don't. But hear me out at least. I used that ticket you left to show up at that Vine event, just out of curiosity. To see your place, to see what you'd built, what you were so passionate about. There was no ulterior motive. It wasn't until I was there that it struck me—that a place like that, that was doing well, that momentum and an amazing, passionate, driven man behind it might still fail without the right financial help. I love our city; I love the Strip District. It's businesses like yours—the small, unique ones—that make Pittsburgh so incredible."

Jeremy found himself still standing there, staring at her hand on the bare skin of his arm.

Darcy barely took a breath, just plowed on. "It occurred to me that this was something I could do. Me— the college dropout who happened to have a knack for making money but no one to share it with and seemingly zero purpose on this earth. I could actually use what I was good at to help somebody other than myself. I was so jazzed, so excited, so—"

She searched his face, but he purposely gave her nothing. He couldn't lose sight of the fact that she'd lied to him, again.

She dropped her hand. "I can't make you understand." Tears still swam in her eyes, but she stuck out her chin and squared her shoulders. "But at least know this: it wasn't about fleecing or tricking you. It wasn't about *you* at all. It was about *me* starting something for myself. Something I could be proud of, something I could do to be a real part of this community, something I could do that would make a difference. You just happened to be my starting place. I thought because you knew me, you might give me a chance."

Jeremy gritted his teeth. "I gave you a chance, all right. Another chance to lie to me."

"I didn't lie!"

"You let me believe—"

"I'm so very sorry, I—"

"The fact is"—Jeremy reached the door and yanked it open—"your silences always speak volumes."

Between their relationship and her increasing involvement in Vine—Jeremy had *finally* come to truly trust her again. But it'd all been a sham. She'd been using him, using Vine, for her own means. He and his club were fucking steppingstones for her never-enough dreams.

"And your silences," he said, "always mean a rash of shit for me." Because this time she'd humiliated him in front of his family and friends. Hell, practically the whole city, given that he now had to call PittsburghHappenings and have them issue a retraction. Anyone who hadn't read the article initially would suddenly be interested.

Darcy wrapped her arms around her middle and shut her eyes.

Jeremy yanked the door shut behind him with a bang—blocking her out of his sight. He bolted for the stairs, taking them two at a time, but he still heard her yell.

"My silences? You always leave—never even able to finish a fight!"

He swore and kept going. He'd tried. He'd risked his heart despite the past. When it came to Darcy, however, it felt like the past always repeated itself. Whether she was disappearing, hiding herself or information about herself, or simply not leveling with him straight out—it didn't matter. He always paid for being with her. And he couldn't do it anymore. He was done.

There was no point in finishing a fight when there was no chance of a future.

24

The next morning, Darcy felt like absolute crap. No surprise there. She'd barely slept, and for once, she couldn't even muster up an appetite. And her regrets—God, the weight of her regrets.

Her father…well, he was her father, and so he'd have to forgive her. He'd always treated her like a child anyway—this would hardly be any different.

As for Jeremy, however, she'd meant to explain early on, but she'd been a coward, choosing to wait for the supposed right timing. Dammit, so stupid. No matter that she hadn't set out to blatantly lie to him, she one hundred percent got that not being entirely up front to suit her own needs was no different from his perspective. As far as he was concerned, she'd flat-out deceived him and betrayed his trust.

So now they were right back at square one—or maybe square negative. He'd walked out in the middle of a fight—if you could call it that—and she had no idea if this had been the last straw. Maybe this time, he wouldn't be able to forgive her? Maybe she'd completely obliterated the trust she'd finally built with him? Maybe he'd never want to lay eyes on her again, and she'd have her answer.

She should have put all her cards—especially the low ones—on the table right off and taken the bigger risk that he might have said no to her investing in Vine. That would have sucked, but at least she'd have been no worse off than she'd been before. Lonely and useless and wealthy.

But not heartbroken. And not the cause of hurt.

Darcy couldn't motivate herself for yoga or even a shower. She alternated between pacing her apartment, staring blankly at the numbers on her computer screen that suddenly made no sense, and checking her phone for messages. Oh, and every once in a while, tears of pure frustration bubbled up out of nowhere, before she forced them away.

Ingrid, her dear housekeeper, somehow managed to clean and hover over her at the same time. Darcy had tried to hide out in her bedroom, but she was too restless.

Finally, Ingrid put her hands on her hips and said, "This is no good. You have to eat something."

Darcy shook her head. "I'm not hungry."

"It doesn't matter. Come." Ingrid fluttered her hand, as if she could dust Darcy right toward the kitchen. Maybe she could, because Darcy found herself there.

Ingrid said, "Sit. Pancakes or eggs?"

Darcy grimaced as she slid onto a kitchen stool at the breakfast bar. "Neither."

"Yogurt with banana?"

"Ewww. Anything mushy is not going to go over well right now."

"Toast it is," Ingrid said. "Now, start talking."

Darcy shook her head.

"When it comes to a man," Ingrid said, "you have to talk to a woman—and us old ones have been around the block."

Darcy gaped.

"Oh, come on, you think I don't notice your change in routine these last couple of months or so? The fact that all the fresh food I brought kept going bad, and your sheets were rarely slept in? Not to mention the smile you couldn't hide." Ingrid shook her head. "I'm not blind. And now? All of the sudden, I see puffy eyes and a red nose. There's heartbreak written all over your face."

"Ingrid…"

"I don't judge, sweetheart," she said. "And I might not even have a peep of decent advice. But I do know that a woman needs to talk a problem out—especially when she can't make sense of things." Ingrid reached across the counter and patted Darcy's linked hands. "And in your case, I happen to also know that you can't even function if you haven't eaten."

Ingrid turned her back, busying herself filling the kettle, sliding bread into the toaster oven, and shifting things in the cupboard until she'd found whatever she'd been searching for.

It was easier to start with Ingrid not staring right at her, and start Darcy did. Right at the beginning—when her college-aged self fell head over heels for a boy who made her feel like she belonged—both at school and in his arms.

By the time she was done with the full story, including the parts she was least proud of, she'd eaten the toast—coated in melted butter, cinnamon, and sugar, because

Ingrid didn't scrimp when it came to comfort food—and the tea had cooled enough to sip.

"Given your background, it's no wonder you thought you had to fudge the truth to score your first client." Ingrid had been with Darcy for her years of testing, assessment, and then tutoring, often serving her tutors cookies and clucking over her like a mother hen.

Darcy winced, horrified because Ingrid was spot-on. Darcy had spent her whole childhood hiding her disability —faking out teachers, compensating wherever necessary, sweeping issues under the rug—as a way to protect herself. Even though she'd made huge strides as an adult in terms of reading fluency, she hadn't—apparently—grown past it emotionally. Her confidence meter apparently was broken way down at *none*. "God, I'm pathetic."

"Hardly," Ingrid scoffed. "You're just regular old human. We make bad calls sometimes that we wish we could take back. But we can't." She set her own cup of tea down on the counter between them. "All we can do is move forward, incorporating what we've learned from our missteps. Oh—and apologize. That's a big one."

"But even if Jeremy lets me get within shouting distance to apologize again, then what?"

"That's the million-dollar question. And the only person that can answer it is you."

Darcy dropped her head into her hands. "That is sooo not helpful."

"I know." Ingrid gave her a gentle smile. "But that's the way it works. In life, the only answer is to follow your heart."

Darcy scowled. Ingrid hadn't been kidding when she said she might not have had an ounce of good advice.

Great insight, yes—ugh—but she wasn't sure that helped her now.

Worse, Darcy suspected Jeremy was the one who got to decide the million-dollar question. She'd choose to be with him every time, no matter the flat-tire-sized potholes in their road. But he might well choose a life without her, because she seemed to always be the one screwing things up.

Ingrid suggested Darcy shower, and between that and the food, Darcy was feeling stronger as she dried off. Still rotten, but at least functioning. She didn't bother with makeup or the hairdryer, just threw on some joggers, a fitted tank, and an off-the-shoulder sweatshirt.

She'd supposed she'd try again to sit at her computer and focus on her monetary concerns rather than her emotional ones. As she exited the bedroom, the house phone rang with the tone that signaled the security desk downstairs.

Darcy's hopes shot forth like a dam had been unplugged—could it be Jeremy? Come to apologize like the last time they'd fought over that damn contract—or at least to finish the discussion for better or worse?

Ingrid was nearer to the kitchen phone and picked up. In a moment, she said, "Pinky says it's your friend Kalpani." She didn't wait for Darcy's approval, only told Pinky to send her up.

Darcy sagged. "What if I didn't feel like a visitor right now?"

"You need people around you," Ingrid said, "and I have to go."

Darcy sighed. "Fine."

Ingrid stowed the granite polish and rag under the

kitchen sink, washed her hands, and then crossed the room to wrap Darcy in a hug. She looked her in the eye and squeezed Darcy's arms in her rough, capable hands.

"It'll all be okay," Ingrid said.

Darcy drew a deep breath.

The elevator chimed, and Ingrid exchanged greetings and places with Kalpani.

"Hi," Darcy said. "Sorry I was a no-show today."

"Well, I wouldn't have worried about it," Kalpani said, "but usually you text, or at least respond."

Darcy winced. "Sorry. Off my game."

"Everything all right?"

She sighed. "Not really."

Kalpani raised an eyebrow. Then she held up a paper bag. "Are savories from 21st Street Coffee and Tea distraction enough?"

"I'm not hungry, but thanks."

"Whoa," she said, "you? Not hungry. Things must be bad."

"They are. Let's get out of this apartment. Want to take a walk? I haven't seen the tree at the Point yet." Pittsburgh's Light Up Night was always the Friday before Thanksgiving and coincided with the Santa Spectacular at Point State Park. She and Jeremy had been too busy to enjoy any of it, and since then…well, she hadn't been feeling festive enough to check out Pittsburgh's many holiday attractions.

By the time they'd bundled up and reached the Point's giant electronic tree—not quite magical, given that those pretty green and red lights didn't have the nighttime backdrop at present—Darcy had spilled pretty much the whole story again. It'd been nearly twenty-four hours since her

Dad had showed up at Vine, but she still felt as horrified as if it had been mere minutes ago.

Like Ingrid, Kalpani had no concrete advice, but Darcy at least felt a bit less alone.

They walked along the promenade, overlooking Pittsburgh's rivers. It was here that the Allegheny and Monongahela rivers met to form the Ohio. From the Point, stunning views of Pittsburgh rose in every direction.

Kalpani said, "So now that you've spilled your beans, and speaking of your investing…"

Darcy slid a glance her friend's way, and Kalpani took a breath that filled her chest. "I have something I've been wanting to ask you, but I'm not sure if this is the best time or the worst."

"Shoot," Darcy said.

"I've long wanted to open my own salon. But—"

"You don't have the capital!" Darcy halted in the middle of the path with a giant grin.

Her friend laughed. "That's not a good thing."

But Darcy's heart leapt. "You need me."

"I need you." Kalpani smiled. "*If* it makes financial sense for both of us."

"Oh my God. This is fantastic." And to Darcy it was. Just because she'd blown things with Jeremy didn't mean she was done. Her relationship might not recover—okay, she wasn't going to think about that right now—but her budding career was still budding. There were other people who needed her. Other people she could help. "Tell me everything."

Kalpani explained that she hadn't planned on opening her own salon for at least another year, but that she'd happened on the perfect building in the Strip District. "It's more expensive than I'd aimed for."

"I assume the location is worth it, though, right?"

"Absolutely—it's got good visibility and there's parking nearby."

They talked more about Kalpani's vision. A hip, full-service salon: stations and sinks on the first floor for hair, quality organic products displayed for sale in a cozy but modern reception area, an office in the rear, and the second-floor rooms would be used for waxing, nail care, and stock. She also hoped to have space upstairs that could be shared between a massage therapist, acupuncturist, reflexologist, and maybe more.

Darcy knew this was the kind of salon women would flock to. Plus, Kalpani was talented—Darcy had been going to her for her own hair for years.

"This building will get snapped up if I don't act fast," Kalpani said. "Plus, I should warn you that I'd need to renovate heavily."

Darcy squeezed her hand. "I'm sure we can make it all work."

Kalpani thanked her with a huge smile, then grimaced. "One problem though, there's a tenant digging in his heels."

"Well, I don't have any experience there, but maybe my lawyer does. Regardless, I'm sure there's options."

"I hope so, but I'm worried. It feels messy."

"Messy how?"

She heaved a sigh. "He's hot." She slid a glance toward Darcy and said, "And I've kissed him."

"Oh my God!" Darcy laughed. "How?"

Kalpani waved her hand. "It's not even worth going into."

Darcy suspected otherwise, but Kalpani obviously wasn't ready to share the juicy details. "Someday I want that story," Darcy said. "But for now, let's head back to my place. I want to get the numbers down."

25

———

Jeremy saw Jonah slink into Vine midway through the last Friday night set. His brother had stationed himself at the bar and was still sitting there after the band packed up and left and the last club goers had gone. The staff just cleaned up around him.

"Go hang out with Jonah," Raven told Jeremy. "He looks like he needs a friend as much as you do."

Jeremy always worked alongside his staff at closing, and tonight he'd been purposely doing a lot of the physical labor—hauling kegs, mopping the floor, anything—as if moving would release some negative energy. But Raven could be onto something. He'd assumed Jonah was here lending support because of the Darcy thing, but maybe there was more to it.

Jeremy slid on to a barstool and clapped Jonah on the shoulder. "Hey, bro."

"Hey," Jonah said. "Good band."

"I only book the good ones," Jeremy said. Although

tonight he wouldn't have known the difference. He wasn't even sure which songs they'd played.

Jonah grunted then swiveled his head toward his older brother. "Dude, that sucked what happened with Darcy and her dad."

Jeremy blew out a breath. "Yeah, thanks." Of course, Jonah had been at the celebration, too.

Wasn't it just fucking great that practically everybody Jeremy cared about had been witness to the incineration of his relationship?

Jesus, he'd been so into Darcy, and it had been going so well that it had felt like the real thing. Meanwhile, it'd all been built on shit, and that shit had exploded in a very public way.

Now that Jeremy was sitting, exhaustion took a front seat. After the debacle, he'd worked the usual long Vine night. Then, having barely processed his anger, he'd hardly slept and done it all over again. Another shift tonight... Yeah, he was fried.

Raven plunked another beer down in front of Jonah and a pint for Jeremy. She added two glasses of water.

"I'm going. Don't do too much damage, guys," she said.

Taking care of him as always. Raven was a good person. Totally straightforward. No games. Why couldn't he fall in love with—

Oh, Christ.

Jeremy was still sitting on the barstool, but he felt like he'd been laid out flat on the hard, cold, beer-wet floor. He gritted his teeth. He'd loved Darcy in college. He admitted he'd never really gotten over her. And it didn't matter one goddamned bit that he'd just realized he *still* loved her. He had to get over it. She wasn't worth loving. Not anymore, and not ever again. He'd wasted his time. So fucking stupid.

He drank a hefty swig of beer. And then another. He looked around his place—this club he'd poured everything into. It'd sucked that he'd needed another cash infusion, but it'd been tolerable, since it'd been from some big company—besides its blond representative—sort of nameless and faceless. Now? Knowing that he was indebted solely to Darcy—a woman he'd trusted but shouldn't have, loved but shouldn't have—that fucking burned.

He heard the door close behind Raven. He blew out a hard breath and forced himself back to the present. Jeremy looked at Jonah. "What's going on with you?"

Jonah shook his head.

They drank their beers in silence for a few minutes.

"Is it a woman?"

"Kind of."

Jeremy snorted. "Kind of? What does that mean? It's a woman who's half alien? Half shark?" Any other night he would have found this damn funny. If Jake had been here, they could have gone on forever making up ridiculous shit to rib Jonah with. Tonight? He didn't really have it in him.

Jonah said, "It means it's not what you think. I'm not in love. I didn't get dumped."

"Or publicly humiliated?"

"Nope," Jonah said, and raised his glass in a salute, "that one's all yours."

"Huh," Jeremy said. "I guess whatever it is, then, you'll live."

"You will too, big bro. You will too."

Well, yeah, Jeremy thought, but the living was going to

suck for a friggin' long time. "So, you came in just to sit beside me and watch me lick my wounds."

"Actually, I did."

"Nice," Jeremy said, and got up to get them both another beer. When he'd set Jonah's in front of him, he said, "So you gonna spill or what? 'Cause it's past my bedtime."

He wasn't only pushing Jonah because it was obvious there was something on his brother's mind. The truth was that Jeremy was dreading going upstairs alone. His apartment held way too many reminders of Darcy—girly shampoo in the shower, a pillow that still held the indent of her head, clothes he knew would hold her scent in his hamper, her half-eaten snacks in the cupboard. Even the air still felt like it held an element of Darcy. He was still angry enough that he had to fight not to open the window and see if he could make some three-pointers: her stuff launched at the dumpster in the back alley. Yet the place also felt uncomfortably depressing without her.

Jonah rolled his shoulders and turned his head to look at Jeremy. "This woman is trying to steal my building."

Jeremy said, "Oh man, that's just wrong. She can't though, right?" Jonah lived and worked in the Strip, too, and if he lost his digs, he'd basically lose his livelihood.

"I wouldn't have thought so, but I'm seriously worried." Jonah gripped his beer bottle like he could stop the world from spinning. "Honestly, it'd be easier to swallow if it was an alien invasion."

"So, give me the old bat's name—"

Jonah gave a bitter laugh. "She's the farthest thing from that."

Jeremy raised his eyebrows and opened his mouth, but Jonah spoke first.

"She's the most beautiful, dynamic, insanely gorgeous woman I've ever met. The worst part is I've kissed her, and all I want is more." He looked at Jeremy, and his eyes showed both misery and excitement.

Jeremy knew that feeling. "Oh, shit."

26

———

Darcy dragged her feet a bit, but on Saturday morning she dragged them all the way to Hellston Investments and made her way up to her dad's office. He nearly always worked Saturday mornings, just without his secretary and office staff, which was ideal for Darcy.

She greeted her father with a kiss on the cheek as he came around the desk. Then apologized right away with the briefest of explanations.

Randolph ruined it by asking, "Why do you want to work, anyway?"

"Because I want to," she said. Old frustrations burst to life again at the non-comprehending look on his face. "Because I want to be good at something and proud of myself. I want to be part of something."

"Well, why didn't you say so? I could've helped you."

"That's not the point, Daddy." She threw out her arms before dropping them to smack the sides of her legs. "And I didn't want your help. Not after all the years of feeling like I wasn't good enough."

"What are you talking about?" His eyebrows drew together in that look—the one that he always wore when he couldn't make sense of his own children.

"Your college dropout? The only one in our whole family who couldn't cut it? The one you didn't want to be a part of Hellston Investments?"

"That's not true," he said. Now his expression showed genuine shock. "I didn't want you to have to struggle with school—or a job—when it was so hard for you. I'm just trying to take care of my girl, give you everything you could want and more."

"Huh," she said softly, at a loss for real words. He had no idea the damage he'd done—she shook her head in amazement—but at least he hadn't done it on purpose.

"I'm still trying," he said. "I'd love to help you with your new venture."

"Thank you," she said, "but this is mine alone. Succeed or fail."

"You'll succeed," he said. "You're smart, intuitive, and obviously motivated."

She had never—*never*—thought to hear those words from her father. The tone wasn't coddling or apologetic. He spoke in his no-nonsense business voice. Darcy's eyes welled up.

"Now, about that Jeremy character," he said.

Good moment over, she thought, and laughed. Her voice wobbled with emotion when she said, "You don't have a say in that either, Daddy."

He crossed his arms and looked at the ceiling like he was pained. Then he looked straight into her eyes. "Does he treat you well?"

"Better than I could have dreamed. He's a good man."

Nothing showed on his face, but he said, "Fine."

"And you might as well know now," she said with a stern look, "I still hope to love him forever, if I haven't blown it past all repair."

"I suppose you don't want my help in that area either?"

Darcy laughed. "No. Definitely not."

Like everything else, she had to own this—mistakes and future both.

———

Early Monday, Darcy left her place to walk the short distance to 21st Street Coffee and Tea. She and Kalpani were meeting to go over some early financial projections for the new salon.

Darcy was relieved to get out of her condo, because mornings were still incredibly tough. Waking alone, feeling such remorse over her mistakes, knowing Jeremy wouldn't be part of her day, dreading another day of disappointment when every ding from a text message wasn't him...

Still, though, she had hope that he just needed to cool down. That he'd miss her enough to call. That he'd maybe realize that yes, she'd made a serious mistake, but that she hadn't done it to hurt him. It was still early, right? Only four and half very, very torturous days since he'd found out that Hellston Enterprises had nothing to do with Hellston Investments.

She reminded herself to be present in her here and now. Even if things weren't great, she should be mindful as she went about her day and recognize things she was grateful for, no matter how small. The fall air was crisp, with the promise of cider and wood fires, and she sucked a cold lungful in. She passed one of her go-to eateries and smiled when she saw the chalkboard touting their weekly specials. They'd added a carved prime rib sandwich with roasted root vegetables, pierogies—one of her favorites— with rosemary, and hot cocoa with peppermint or eggnog flavoring. 'Twas the season—the calendar had officially flipped to December. She'd be sure to come back in the next couple of days.

There was something big, too, that she was incredibly grateful for: despite being battered romantically, she'd been bolstered in another way. Knowing her dad didn't think she was an embarrassment and failure—a marvel in itself—was oddly freeing. Like a whole suitcase of old baggage, heavy as bricks, had been magically replaced with a snazzy new briefcase of the finest leather and a pass key that could open any door.

She knew in her heart that helping Kalpani would lead to another opportunity and another. She was excited and confident and pumped. She'd polish her skills and increase her knowledge base at each new venture, and become more than just the money source, but a true partner in success in every project she took on.

Unlike her venture with Jeremy. She'd failed him. Big time. Damn, but that was brutally painful to admit. She'd let her hang-ups and their relationship get in the way of being an honest businessperson. She was finally owning it. There just wasn't anything to do about it.

She'd put everything on the line when she'd proposi- tioned him for a full-on relationship. She still wanted that. Still wanted him. Truly, spending her future with Jeremy was—still—what she wanted more than anything in the world.

Ingrid had suggested Darcy follow her heart. But right now, she was pretty sure knocking on his door would be like banging her head against a brick wall. The sound wouldn't get through, and she'd be far worse for wear.

Jeremy was going to forgive her or he wasn't, and that ball—unfortunately—was in his court.

She spotted Kalpani and weaved through the tables. Another entry in the gratefulness column: a trusted friend.

"Hi." She smiled and slid into the seat across from her friend, noting that a coffee awaited her. "Did you already order?"

Kalpani nodded. "All the usuals. It'll be up in a minute."

Darcy thanked her, placed the Hellston Enterprises folder on the table, and pulled her tablet out of her bag. A thrill shot through her as she explained her research to Kalpani, and that enthusiasm grew as they talked and ate their way through a scrumptious breakfast.

When they'd covered everything, Kalpani said, "Thanks again. I'm so grateful, I—"

"Please." Darcy shook her head. "I'm thrilled to be able to help, and it's great for my own business, too."

And that was pure awesome fact. She was on her way, and who knew how many businesses she'd be able to give a leg up?

She wouldn't be able to take on every case, of course. Nor would every venture be successful. Some promising ventures might even fail miserably despite her best efforts…

Much like the mess she'd made of her relationship

with Jeremy, which might not be possible to salvage. She took a deep breath, owning the regret.

She'd likely have to find a way to live with that. And at least there was some solace in the fact that she had helped his business. She'd provided cash, advice, new ideas—all of which had been a success. And as for her investment—Jeremy would likely pay off his debt to Hellston Enterprises as Vine became solvent faster than originally agreed. But even if he defaulted, she didn't care. There'd be no penalty or repercussion from her.

Kalpani chattered away, and Darcy noted her excited tone and the glow on her face—all because of this new opportunity. Darcy was already invested emotionally, too. She'd committed herself nearly the minute her friend had mentioned it, and she wouldn't quit halfway. Or ever.

Wait a minute... Vine shouldn't be any different. She'd been forced to take a step back, given the demise of their relationship. Still... Darcy thought about the ideas she'd discussed with Jeremy, the ones they hadn't yet had time to try. She smiled.

"What?" Kalpani asked.

"Nothing," she told her, wanting to keep today's focus on Kalpani's dreams.

But it was hardly nothing. It was a big, good, important something. She could still honor her commitment and—as Ingrid so wisely advised—follow her heart where Jeremy and Vine were concerned. She'd simply be doing it from a distance.

27

———

On the second Wednesday in December, Jeremy was cranking through some paperwork in the office. Now that he had the turntable in his apartment, he'd brought the small wireless speaker he had been using down to his office. He cranked some old Pearl Jam, in the mood for some Seattle grunge. Tunes definitely made these tasks more palatable, and, seemingly, he accomplished more. He had about an hour before tonight's staff started to arrive.

His phone rang with an unknown number, and he answered it.

The man on the other end said, "This is Brad Rynkiewicz from Steel City Brewery. Darcy Hellston recommended I talk to you."

Jeremy stilled. *Interesting*.

There was no easy way to turn the music down, given that the app he used was on the phone, so he stepped out of the office. "What can I do for you, Brad?"

"She mentioned you might be up for carrying some of

our seasonal brews on tap and that you might have need of flights during some events."

"That's right," Jeremy said. "A tap takeover could work, too." Rarely able to stand still when he talked on the phone, he pushed through the door and entered the larger space of Vine, as he and Brad talked through the possibilities of partnering up once in a while.

Raven was already here, and she raised an eyebrow. He mouthed, *Steel City Brewery,* and she gave him a thumbs-up and a pleased look.

When they were through, he thought they'd struck a nice balance—both Vine and Steel City Brewery should benefit. He hung up and looked at Raven.

"Nice work," she said. "The owner of Steel City?"

He shook his head. "Yeah, Brad. But he called me. Darcy suggested it to him."

She raised both black eyebrows sky high.

He rubbed a hand over his face, then shook his head. "Back to it. I'll come help you in a few."

He'd no sooner settled back into his paperwork when Raven poked her head in.

"You've got visitors."

Jeremy pushed up from the desk. Eddie Vedder's blasting vocals meant he hadn't heard the door. Excitement mingled with dread—and yet if Darcy hadn't come by now, she wasn't going to, was she? Did he even want her to? Yes, if he was honest—because there was a gaping hole in his life without her. And no because—well, a lot of damn good reasons.

He followed Raven into the hallway and heard voices —men's voices. Raven had said visitors, plural. Not Darcy.

"Who is it?"

"You'll see," she said with a grin.

He blew out a breath. He wasn't in the mood to play games. But his tune changed when he saw who graced his dance floor. Danny Blake and his band—a well-known, killing-it, charting band—stood there shooting the shit.

"Guys, meet Jeremy," Raven said. "Jeremy, meet the Danny Blake Band."

Jeremy greeted each by name, shaking hands, starting with Danny. They'd headlined at the Freeze Fest at Point State Park over the weekend. One of the rare events this time of year that had nada to do with the holiday, it catered to a non-family crowd—college kids, twenty-somethings, and music-lovers that ran the age gamut. Everyone bundled up and snuggled on blankets or danced to keep warm. They sold spiked cider and hot chocolate, or flavored freezies for the daring set.

Jeremy had taken a few hours out, taking a page from Darcy's book, and gone down there with his winter coat, ski hat, and a thick blanket to enjoy the tail end of the festival. But the Danny Blake Band had played Saturday night, so Jeremy hadn't seen them. In fact, Vine's Saturday night headcount had been decidedly low because of the Freeze Fest.

Raven, who usually kept an eye on things from behind the bar or as she went in and out of the storage room, stayed put. Apparently, there was no way she was willing to miss whatever this was.

"So, what can I do for you?" Jeremy asked, with anticipation tingling. Should he even hope...

"Pretty simple, really," Danny said. "We want to do a gig at Vine once in a while."

"If his ego can still fit on a stage that size," Carey said, and they all laughed. Danny raised his chin at his bandmate's dig.

Jeremy had time to form a response and still couldn't manage anything impressive. He turned up his hands. "Yes. Hell yes." More chuckles as he recovered. "That'd be great. What kind of timing are you looking at?"

After they'd covered that ground, Jeremy said, "So how'd you hear about Vine?"

"Simon here is from Aspinwall."

"Right." Jeremy had known Simon was from that area of Pittsburgh. "But Vine didn't even exist back then."

"He misses his momma," Carey said with an elbow to the ribs. Jeremy and Raven chuckled along with the band. It was nice to see a band who still enjoyed each other after the pressure of fame had touched them.

"Seriously, man," Danny said, "we'd been talking about missing our roots—you know, not a specific place, but like it used to be when we were still coming up. The familiarity of playing somewhere you knew, the intimacy of playing to a small crowd." He shrugged. "We want the option to play what the hell we want sometimes, not what our agent wants, or the ticket price demands. But we didn't want to do it just anywhere."

Rich added, "We saw you, hanging at the festival, chilling out." He looked at the other guys who were nodding along. "You know, really listening, man."

Simon interjected, "My nephews had mentioned Vine, so your blanket caught my eye."

Jeremy's mom had given him that blanket when Vine had opened—it had a huge club logo on it.

"Then," Simon continued, "when we read up, we realized it was you we'd seen. And we figured you'd run the kind of place that was about the music—not just the names or the revenue."

"I'm—" Wow, Jeremy was…

"He's honored," Raven said, and they laughed again.

After Jeremy escorted the band out, he strode back down the corridor. He was so stoked he wanted to run or leap like friggin' Peter Pan. Maybe even fly.

He headed directly for Raven. He could hear her in the storeroom.

"Holy shit," he said.

Her grin was ear to ear. "I know!"

"We're going to have a line down the street." He shook his head, wide-eyed. "But I don't even care about that—it's just so cool."

"It's amazing," she said. "To think they chose Vine because you went to that festival. Actually took time out to chill. You got business from *not* working."

"Crazy."

"Crazy," she agreed. "And…"

"And what?" He frowned.

"And who suggested you take time to listen to music now and then?"

He rolled his eyes. "Darcy suggested I find a way to relax. I decided to go to the festival on my own." He didn't admit that he'd heard her voice in his head, pushing him to go and enjoy when he'd been worried about getting behind on work.

"Uh-huh," Raven said. "And would the guy from Steel City Brewery have called if Darcy hadn't reached out to him?"

He widened his stance and gave Raven a dirty look—not that she'd pay a bit of attention to it.

"Hmm," she said, making a big show of looking wide-eyed with surprise. "Didn't that Veronica woman with the serious vocal chops show up because of Darcy?"

He heaved a sigh and inclined his head. Yes, Darcy had sent her, and hell yes, the blues singer was so damn good that he'd made sure to sign her for multiple dates.

Jeremy crossed his arms. "You forgot one."

Raven snapped her fingers. "So I did. That food truck guy we used during the other night's Latin Lounge? Man, was his stuff tasty."

Jeremy admitted that the food had been damn good and the price point reasonable. Plus, the dude had been ultra-professional, and he'd brought enough of his own people that Jeremy had barely needed his own.

Raven put her hands on her hips. "What was that fight you two had even about again?"

———

Vine was jammed, and Jeremy had taken over the taps at the back of the bar, facing away from the crowd and band. Raven stood behind him, face out, dealing with people. Exactly what he needed tonight, because his mind was only half present. Between the Danny Blake Band's surprise visit and Raven's not so subtle set-down—curse her—Jeremy couldn't stop thinking about the bigger picture. Look what happened when he backed off? When he was true to why he'd started this kind of business in the first place?

He'd landed one of the hottest bands in the Northeast.

He shook his head as he poured drafts and packed as many as would fit comfortably on one of his server's trays. She returned, and he spread his palm over the three to the left. "These are the lites." He pointed to another. "This one's the Killian."

She nodded, bent her knees to slide the tray from the bar, and then up it went as she threaded her way around the rest of the staff and out into the crowd. Right behind her came the next server, and he automatically processed that verbal order as he grabbed pint glasses. Jeremy let tonight's hip sound wash past him as he poured.

When Raven stacked up all those events a few hours ago like so many building blocks, it made him realize... Darcy was good for him. Every which way, ten times to Sunday. And it wasn't just about great sex, some intertwined history, and a comfort level with each other. She cared for him, she supported him, and she pushed him in good ways. She'd signed on to help him with Vine. But he knew that for her, it wasn't just about Vine's financial success. It never really had been—she'd wanted *him* to succeed as a business owner. But she'd also pushed him as a person to be whole and happy.

Another server plopped her tray down next to him. Getting his most soft-spoken server to speak louder failed every time. So, he simply leaned in, aiming his ear directly at her mouth.

"Come again?" he said. She repeated the order, and he nodded.

Darcy, Jeremy thought once his hands were occupied again, was one hundred percent right that life couldn't be all about his business. That there had to be time out for just living. Yeah, there was listening to music, working out, seeing his brothers and his mom. But aiming for balance didn't hold nearly the appeal without Darcy in the picture.

Jeremy had a brief reprieve between orders and turned around to survey the scene. Servers were hustling, Raven was a whirling dervish as always, the crowd was dancing and jumping—but well behaved.

A shrill whistle cut through the blaring bass, causing Jeremy to look left toward the front hallway that fed toward the bar. His bouncer, Alberto, gave him the high sign. They'd reached capacity. Jeremy returned a thumbs-up and a grin. All was well with his world—well, the slice of it that constituted Vine, anyway.

He allowed himself to watch the band, soaking up the music for a few minutes. Then, before he'd had a chance to put the brakes on, he was envisioning time spent with Darcy. Lazy mornings in bed when they'd reach for each other, cooking her dinner while she clicked her way through pages and pages of spreadsheets on her big moni-tors, walking arm in arm through the Strip to visit his family at The Wanderlust, lying on the lawn for outdoor music festivals with her head on his shoulder, trips to all the 'Burgh neighborhoods to fulfill her food cravings... Hell, he'd even suffer charity balls and golf outings with her father if that was what she wanted.

Holy hell. He actually would. Gladly.

It seemed that despite her omission of important details and the shit that followed—a life that included Darcy was *still* what he wanted.

Imperfect and amazing, sexy and stunning, caring and giving, smart and driven Darcy. *She* was what he wanted.

Of course, now he had to prove it—if she was even still willing to listen.

28

Darcy had made some changes over the last few weeks. She had found a sub for the last two matches of her indoor tennis league and had also let the group know she wouldn't be able to play in the spring. It was all the same people she saw at the club for golf, anyway, and Jeremy had been right. It wasn't that fun. She added in another yoga class. She also declined two charity events she would normally have accepted without a second thought, opting to send a donation to each instead. She corralled Kalpani and a couple of others from the yoga studio to go listen to some music—just not at Vine. And she spent many hours researching the salon business in order to give Kalpani the best leg up she could.

But the fact was that there was a damn big hole in her heart and in her life. Next week was Christmas. Not only was she not spending it with Jeremy, her heart still clung to what could have been, if only she'd laid all her cards on the table from the beginning. As far as romantic relationships went, she'd only ever loved him. She simply couldn't imagine ever finding someone who would compare. She didn't particularly want a solitary life, but she didn't want just anyone taking up space, either. She wanted Jeremy.

And yet, knocking on Jeremy's door with her tail tucked and heart on her sleeve and a pleading look on her face? She simply couldn't do it. Because she already had. She'd offered her heart and soul, offered him her whole future.

If he called? Now that was another story. But he didn't, and the days and nights had added up to weeks, and Darcy had lost hope.

She stepped off her elevator, dropped her purse, toed off her shoes, and just stood there. She used to feel such comfort when she arrived home to her beautiful apartment. But her sanctuary no longer held the same sense of peace. Ingrid had been here—Darcy could smell the fresh scent of cleaning products. But now it was too quiet and too tidy, only amplifying her loneliness.

Her shoulders slumped. Some days were harder than others. A few days ago, she drove to Jeremy's apartment to retrieve the clothes and makeup she'd left there, then decided better of it and left before getting out of the car.

Her possessions were only things. Things she could replace. But if she removed those things and left her key on his kitchen counter? That would have become a state-ment signifying that she was done, that she was closing their relationship officially—and that she couldn't do either, not even to salvage her pride.

No matter that he was done. She wasn't done. She would never be done. Jeremy was the only man she ever loved or ever wanted to love.

Darcy heaved a sigh and finally crossed to the bedroom to change her clothes. A headache was brewing, so she rummaged in the bathroom cabinet but couldn't find the ibuprofen. Where had she used it last? Oh yes, her nightstand. She'd ended up with a headache in the middle of the night a couple of times with all the crying herself to sleep she'd done lately.

Darcy yanked open the drawer and stopped short.

Ages ago, she'd propped up the old event ticket to Vine on her nightstand, but at some point, either Ingrid or she had tucked it away. It was the one that Jeremy had left her in True Springs, the one that had shocked her when she'd picked it up.

Of course, she'd been upset that day, too. They'd spent that amazing night together at the Sweetwater Inn—and then to have it end so awfully, her fears tying her tongue. Of course he'd been quick to assume the worst after the way she'd abandoned him in college.

Somehow, she was always blowing it with Jeremy, always left feeling low.

She reached for the event ticket and fingered it. Just a regular piece of heavy cardstock with that rip down the side the bouncers had given it when she'd entered. Long before she knew Alberto and Steve personally.

Things *had* changed, though. Starting on the very night she'd decided to use this ticket and check out Vine—the night her big idea was born, the one that set her on a whole new path for her life.

She hadn't managed to hang on to Jeremy, but she had that.

She rubbed her thumb over Vine's logo and wondered how it was going. She knew from some thank-yous she'd received that Jeremy had been receptive to the various vendors she'd suggested contact him. She wished her actions had prompted Jeremy to reach out to her, but apparently his mind was made up.

She blew out a breath. She hadn't sent people his way for that reason—she'd committed to Vine's success period —but, of course, she couldn't help hoping, either.

She set the ticket on the nightstand. She'd put it in her office later. Maybe she'd buy a bulletin board, or maybe she'd just tuck it among her new business files. No matter that it had come from Jeremy, it signified a new beginning, and so much more for her personally and professionally.

Beyond that, she'd really have to—somehow—learn to accept the fact that there would be no future with Jeremy. Darcy shut her eyes and shook her head. Then she dug out the ibuprofen and crossed to the bathroom for water.

She still hadn't totally regained her usual appetite, but suspected food might also help her head. She headed for the kitchen to see if Ingrid had left anything good.

The woman was a saint, always depositing pints of soup or containers of delicious leftovers, right along with some fresh groceries. That was another thing. Without Jeremy to enjoy it with, Darcy's newfound, albeit basic, cooking skills languished.

Ingrid had stacked the mail on the counter, and a large courier envelope caught Darcy's eye.

She picked it up and turned it over. To Ms. Darcy Hell-ston, yep. From—

The address was Vine's—Jeremy's.

Darcy's skin erupted in goosebumps—half thrill, half dread. Always with Jeremy she dreamed, hoped, ached, but the feasible reasons for sending something in this manner were all rotten. She stood stock-still, staring at the envelope. Had he written her a final Dear John letter—as if his silence hadn't been telling enough? Had he sent some sort of legal rescindment of their original contract? Or maybe he'd mailed a check, paying all the money he owed —effectively ending the last tie she had to him.

Finally, she clasped the envelope to her chest and shut her eyes.

"Please," she whispered to God and any and all universal forces who might take pity on her already fragile heart, "something good."

Then she opened her eyes and raised her chin as she sucked in a sustaining breath—and tore the pull tab clean off.

She peered inside, breathing shallowly, seeing mostly just the interior cardboard color of the envelope—but there at the bottom…

Reaching inside, she pulled out a ticket—no more than five or six inches long and two inches tall. A sticky note was attached.

In Jeremy's tiny chicken scratch, it said, *I put you down as my guest. Just show up if you can make it.*

He had signed only "J." No "love" or "thanks" or "please."

She hadn't realized that she'd stopped breathing until she gasped and her heart beat double time briefly before settling down.

She peeled the note away. The ticket was for an Annual Casino Night—tomorrow evening—hosted by the Strip District Development and Preservation Association, or SDDPA. She sprinted to her office, popped her password into her computer, and waited impatiently for her normally quick browser to load. She searched for the group's website and the event and skimmed the information. It appeared to be a combination fundraiser and networking.

A nasty thought crossed her mind. Had Jeremy thought of her—Ms. Moneybags—because of the fundraising?

No. Surely, he'd realize this kind of event would be good for her personal goal of seeking out other business owners she could help... A good thing, right? And he'd said she'd be his guest—which was also telling, wasn't it?

She was afraid to read too much into it, afraid to even smile about it...but hope took root, no matter how much she warned her yearning heart against it.

Tomorrow night. She wouldn't miss it for anything—come what may.

29

Casino Night was held at the beautiful Renaissance Pittsburgh Hotel in the historic Fulton Building. Darcy had actually been there for two other events in the last six months, but she'd never tire of the grand lobby with its castlelike staircase and iconic domed ceiling.

There was a small backup at the door of the Symphony Ballroom. A man in a tux with a bushy mustache made a big show of tearing each ticket, placing the end in a big clear ball—just like on TV—and giving it a spin with quite a flourish. He instructed the stub holder to be sure to keep the other half in case the number was called as a winner later. He then proceeded to count out chips: two hundred and fifty "dollars." More than the cost of each ticket, but not by much.

By the time it was her turn, Jeremy appeared. He looked amazing, all dressed up in a button-down and slacks, offset by his sexy scruff. But she'd have been just as happy to see him in a t-shirt and jeans. God, she'd missed him.

Darcy smiled, nerves tumbling over themselves like the paper pieces in that ball. She smoothed her scarf, even as she held out her ticket. She reminded herself that he'd invited her. That had to mean a chance at forgiveness at least, right?

"Be careful with that one," Jeremy told the man, indicating her ticket. "The thing shocked me when I mailed it." His tentative smile was directed at her, though, and she warmed despite the cautionary refrain in her head. *It doesn't mean anything, not yet.*

"The air's been so dry," the grandmaster said, taking Darcy's ticket. "Ah, nope. It's lost its charge now."

Darcy lowered one eyebrow. That was weird. Her ticket to the Vine event way back when had shocked her. This one had apparently shocked him. What in the world were they putting in paper these days? Something more than trees, that was for sure.

After she'd patiently suffered through the tux guy's spiel, acting as if she was hearing it for the first time, she moved forward into the room. Jeremy fell into step beside her.

"That guy needs an assistant," she said, by way of an icebreaker.

"No kidding," Jeremy said. He gave her a sidelong glance. "Thanks for coming. Our seats are over here."

They passed tables—not yet in play—for roulette, craps, and blackjack. She wasn't much of a gambler, preferring proven investment strategies for monetary gain, but she knew the basics.

The drapes were open to a gorgeous evening view of Pittsburgh's famed Three Sisters Bridges and PNC Park beyond. Their table was toward the back of the room, and

Jeremy indicated which seat was hers. A glass of white wine waited there for her.

"White's still good?" he asked, looking worried.

"Yes, thank you." Even if her preferences had changed over the last month, she wouldn't have admitted it.

Several people stood chatting nearby, and Jeremy introduced her to all of them. "She invests in small businesses. Really knows her stuff," he told them.

Darcy's heart swelled. If she hadn't already been in love with him, that would have done it.

This group of folks were mainly owners of businesses in the Strip District: a man who owned the candy shop, a woman who had an imports business, a councilwoman, and a couple who owned B.B. Mac's.

"Oh," Darcy exclaimed, realizing why they looked so familiar, "I love your food!" Theirs was one of her favorites, and in fact it was where she and Jeremy had ordered takeout from the night they'd begun their relationship.

"She's not kidding," Jeremy said. "She might be solely responsible for keeping you in business."

She elbowed him in the ribs, and Jeremy laughed—a genuine laugh. She still didn't know where they stood, but he could tease her all he wanted if he'd just keep smiling at her. It was helping her nerves settle.

She struck up a conversation with the couple, peppering them with questions about how long they'd had the business and how they'd come by their mouth-watering recipes. She heard the candy shop man ask Jeremy how his mom was doing after his dad's passing.

Everyone sat and sipped their drinks while the SDDPA event coordinator said a few remarks about the organization's mission and the goals of tonight's event. The parameters of tonight's gaming were explained, and then it was time to socialize and gamble for a good cause.

Jeremy stayed by Darcy's side all evening, slipping her his chips when she'd lost her own, introducing her to one person after another, making sure she didn't want for drinks or food.

Darcy's insecurity thawed under the attention he lavished on her. She became convinced tonight was an apology of sorts, and finally she allowed herself to truly hope that she and Jeremy might yet have a future together.

Neither of them won anything during the lottery, but one of their tablemates scored seats to a Steelers game. Then the serving staff brought plates of mini pastries and cookies to the table and began offering coffee.

Jeremy turned to her. "Want to skip out—maybe take a walk with me?"

Her heart rate bumped up another notch. "Sure," she said, and reached for her jacket from the back of the chair. She straightened the small stack of business cards she'd received from all the people Jeremy had introduced her to and zipped them inside her wristlet. She'd already tucked away her non-winning ticket stub. She sensed she'd won something far more important than game tickets or a massage or a restaurant voucher—it was just yet to be seen exactly what. Hopefully another chance…

After they said their goodbyes, they made their way to the beautiful lobby. Darcy tried not to think of the numerous weddings she'd attended in that stunning space. There were levels of hopeful, and she'd been crushed enough to want to keep her expectations reasonable.

When they finally exited the hotel, she said, "Thanks again for inviting me. This was really great."

Jeremy inclined his head. "I know how important to you growing your investment business is. You've done wonders for Vine, and you'll be great for others down the road."

"Thank you," Darcy said, feeling incredibly touched, even as her stomach sank. Was tonight all just business for him, then?

"Seriously, you've been amazing, even…since… well…" He ran a hand through his hair before shoving it in his pocket. "Despite what happened—"

She stopped in the middle of the sidewalk. "Jeremy, I'm so sorry."

"I know. I really do. And it's okay." He flashed her a wry but fleeting smile. "I get that sometimes we choose courses of action that we think better of later." He held out a hand.

Now her stomach leapt and settled like when a car went airborne for a second. What a night of ups and downs. Oh, how she wished she knew what he was thinking. What did it mean to hold hands now?

Darcy reached out and slipped her hand in his. The furrow between his brow cleared and a small smile appeared on his face. They walked with hands clasped toward the Roberto Clemente Bridge.

On Pirates game days, the city closed the bridge to auto traffic, but that wasn't the case tonight. The rush of cars accompanied them as they entered the pedestrian walk of the bridge, and so it was easy to walk in silence. It was dark and cool, but the lamps on the bridge glowed and the lights of PNC Park and the North Shore twinkled ahead.

After a couple of minutes, Jeremy cleared his throat. "Speaking of actions we're not proud of…"

She looked at him. He winced, but held her eyes as they walked. "I should never have let you go." He squeezed her hand. "I should have come after you, or called, or, I don't know—at least attempted to save what we had."

Darcy took a deep breath, and that hope that had grown throughout the evening bubbled up into her chest and burst free.

He stopped right there over the Allegheny River to face her, taking both her hands in his. That furrow was back in his brow. "I should never have just given up," he said. "I miss you. Even though things have been busy and so much is going right—largely because of you still working for Vine even though I've been such an ass—I feel like none of it really matters without you."

Tears welled in her eyes—she knew exactly what he meant, but she'd never in a million years thought he'd be saying it out loud.

He pulled back with a pained expression and dropped her hands. "I'm too late."

She was torn between a sob and a laugh. She snatched his big hands back and squeezed them. "No. Not too late." Her voice was wobbly with emotion.

He leaned his forehead against hers. "Christ, you scared me."

Tears spilled over then—she was so full of relief and emotion. She put her hands on his face and pressed her lips to his in a salty kiss. Then she pulled back just enough so that he could see her eyes. "What I told you that night I pushed us toward a full-fledged relationship will always be true. I've always loved you, and I always will. No matter how many missteps we each make, you are the only man for me."

"I love you too," he said, and this time he smiled—one of his very rare, from-the-inside-out smiles. "Never stopped—even when I pretended I didn't."

They grinned at each other like loons. He pressed a tender kiss to her lips, and then smoothed the tear tracks from her cheeks.

He said, "I think we should go back to True Springs—both a do-over and a celebration." Her hair blew wildly in the wind, and he smoothed it back from her face holding it in place.

"That sounds wonderful," she said, grasping his wrists. "A romantic weekend to kiss and make up for lost time."

"Or," he said, "maybe something a little more formal."

A bolt of electric joy shot through Darcy. Was he—

"How would you feel about making it official?" Jeremy clasped her hands in his. "Because I don't want to waste another minute." And then, right there in the middle of the Roberto Clemente Bridge's pedestrian walkway, he sank to one knee.

Darcy's mouth dropped and her eyes sprang wide. "Oh my God."

"Darcy Hellston, will you marry me?"

"Yes! Yes, I will marry you, Jeremy Walker." She launched herself at him. He stood, lifting her off her feet for a second. And then Darcy kissed him with all the love she felt—love that had multiplied exponentially from the first kiss they'd shared as college kids.

When they came up for air, he was grinning. Then he

seemed to sober. "Only thing is, I don't have a ring for you yet."

"I don't care," she said. "Wait—I don't need one. As my father's only daughter, I'll get my grandmother's engagement ring."

"If that's what you want." He narrowed his eyes. "But the wedding band will be from me. No arguments."

She laughed. "Deal. No paperwork necessary."

————

Thank you for reading *Second Chance Love Affair*! Are you wishing you could spend just a little more time with Jeremy and Darcy? Do you need the juicy details of their magical rollercoaster of a weekend that precedes this book? A short prequel is available exclusively to my email subscribers for FREE! Subscribe via my website: www.jbschroederauthor.com

Ready to dive into the youngest Walker brother's full story? Jonah is finally getting his life on track—that is until Kalpani buys the building he believes is his, right out from under him. She's married to growing her business. Somehow, someway, Jonah has to prove that he's the best partner ever—an asset Kalpani can't possibly live without…

Turn the page for a sneak peek—or order
Dreaming of Forever with You now!

DREAMING OF FOREVER WITH YOU

Chapter 1

The bell above the Print & Ship's door wasn't enough to pull Jonah Walker's attention from his creation on the oversized computer screen, but the lilt of Indian voices made his head jolt up.

It wasn't Sohel, of course. The old man had died just a week and a half ago, but the funeral hadn't been held yet, so it was hard to even believe he was truly gone. Sohel's presence in this shop had been such a constant over the years, and his influence on Jonah had been nearly as strong as that of his own father. Jonah wavered between denial and missing Sohel like hell. It didn't help that Jonah had lost his father less than a year ago and had barely come to terms with that.

These visitors were a man and a woman. Sohel's shop —now Jonah's—was a full-service print shop and shipping outlet. Sohel, with Jonah's help in his later years, had done it all: from scanning documents to designing business cards, from xeroxing copies to printing large-scale banners, from selling packing tape to shipping internationally. With all the recent changes in technology, some of their services were rarely sought out these days, while others would likely always be needed. More and more lately, however, it was common for folks to poke their heads in to ask about the art in the window.

This young, well-dressed couple wasn't even looking at Jonah, however.

Their backs were to him and they were chatting among themselves in what Jonah thought of as Inglish—half Indian and half English. What *were* they doing? Inspecting the ceiling and the walls?

Jonah stood and approached the counter before clearing his throat. "Can I help you?"

The couple turned and—

Whoa. Jonah's heart thumped hard even as his body tensed. Because standing in front of him was the woman he'd kissed—like, a whole year ago—and hadn't been able to get out of his mind since.

"Jonah, isn't it?"

Excellent. She apparently hadn't suffered the same fate, if she wasn't even sure of his name.

He nodded. "Kalpani," he said, trying to avoid any inflection. He'd loved the way her name rolled off his lips. He'd said it over and over again that night. As he kissed her neck, her jaw, her lips… She'd been dressed in a traditional sari then, whereas now she wore skinny black pants, a hot-pink blouse, short-heeled boots, and a tailored, nubby winter coat. She was no less gorgeous.

Jonah came around the counter and approached them. "I'm sorry about Sohel. I understand the funeral is Friday."

"Thanks. Condolences to you as well." Her dark eyes darted away. "Yes. And there's a luncheon after at the community center."

The very same community center they'd snuck out back of to make out like teenagers and talk until morning. Hadn't mattered that he was twenty-seven—he'd just wanted to get the long-haired, petite beauty with the mischievous eyes and kissable lips alone.

"This is my cousin, Ajay," Kalpani said.

Ajay nodded, but his smile was fake. He pulled a business card from the back pocket of his fitted slacks and extended it to Jonah with two fingers, then he rocked back on his shiny shoes and shoved his thumbs in his pockets.

Jonah looked at the card. Dude was a real estate agent. *Nice.* Jonah had just finally come into owning something —the first thing ever, and it just happened to be a prime piece of property in the 'burgh's hopping Strip District— and already the vultures were circling.

"I'm not interested in selling," Jonah said, and extended the card back to Ajay.

His eyebrows rose, but Kalpani's mouth dropped open. She said, "Excuse me?"

Ajay hadn't taken the card, so Jonah let it fall to the floor. He crossed his arms. "You heard me."

"But what do you mean?" she said.

"Just what I said. I'm not selling. So you and your cousin can stop eyeballing my building and go find some other listing and client to harass."

If possible, Kalpani's jaw dropped further.

Ajay gave him a placating smile. "I think there's been a misunderstanding. This building is for sale. I'm representing it—"

What the fuck? "Like hell—"

"Wait," Kalpani said, throwing a hand out. "Didn't Uncle Sohel's lawyer contact you?"

Kalpani wasn't directly related to Sohel, but all the elder men in her culture were referred to as uncles by the younger generations, related or not. Even as Jonah's mind darted through the labyrinth of Sohel's network of family and friends, a sinking feeling settled in his gut.

"No. Sohel's not even buried yet, remember?" Jonah uncrossed his arms—subconsciously needing them free, bracing for a fight.

Kalpani shut her eyes and shook her head. She sucked in a deep breath and pinned him with a hard, heated look— an entirely different kind of heat than she'd graced him with last year, when her hands had slid into his hair and she'd pulled his head down for a mind-melting lip-lock.

"Uncle Sohel's estate—in its entirety—was left to his family."

Jonah blinked rapidly as if moving his eyelids would make sense of that statement. "No," he said. "No, he left the shop to me."

She shook her head. "That's simply untrue."

"He showed me the will," Jonah said, probably too loud.

"Look," Kalpani said, her nostrils flaring, "I don't know what you are trying to pull, but you can cut the bull-shit right now. The Gupta family now owns this property, they've asked Ajay to sell it, and I will be buying it. Period."

"Get out," Jonah said.

The cousins stared at him.

"Get. Out." Jonah lunged forward, and finally the duo

burst into action, spinning away from him. Ajay put his arm around Kalpani as if to protect her as they hustled for the door.

The bell jangled happily even though they yanked the door hard. The sounds of pedestrian traffic flowed in as it swung shut ever so slowly.

Then Jonah was left with only the sounds of his own ragged breathing. Worse was the growing fear that despite all his hard work, dedication, and promises made, he'd just lost everything.

Hope you enjoyed this sneak peek and will read
Dreaming of Forever with You right away!

Love That Lasts series:

Faking It Together (#1)
Second Chance Love Affair (#2)
Dreaming of Forever with You (#3)
Starting Over Together (#4)
and
Making Forever with You (Prequel
—co-authored with Savannah Kade!)

THANKS AND MORE

I'm so thrilled you found *Second Chance Love Affair*! Would you kindly share your enjoyment of the story by leaving a brief review on Goodreads, BookBub, or your retailer? Reviews and word of mouth (*please do tell a friend!*) are still the best way for readers to find books they'll love. So grateful for each and every review —thank you!

I love to hear from readers, and these days there are so many ways for us to connect! On my website (www.jbschroederauthor.com), you can subscribe to my newsletter to have news delivered right to your email inbox or visit the Finding JB page to reach me via my social media links—choose what works for you. If you prefer *only* new release alerts, however, simply follow me on BookBub or Amazon.

ACKNOWLEDGMENTS

Every book truly takes a village, and I'm so grateful to mine:

Kate Schroeder: My blessing, my love, and my good fortune that you have a special gift for brainstorming names and titles! Especially for difficult letters like V. Um, can you please start thinking about X!?

Deb Garlock: I'm so lucky to have you as my boots on the ground in the Strip! Thank you for the supply of amazing photos and always providing the most wonderfully knowledgeable responses to my questions.

Ann Marie Browne: Dear friend—thank you for a lovely lunch, candid conversation, and excellent research suggestions.

Linda Auld: Managing director of the Suburban Learning Center in Maplewood, NJ. Thank you for sharing your time and thirty years of expertise with a lone author just trying to get it right!

Hector Ojeda: Workmate and now friend. Thanks for

always fielding my crazy research questions without batting an eye.

Christi Snow, Savannah Kade, and Eli Collier: Your suggestions were gold! Thank you for putting so much time and effort into my work—I owe you a whole treasure chest.

Arran McNicol, editor, and Jen Coleman, proofreader: you two can't be beat for excellence and speed! So glad to have found you!

My readers: always, always, huge love!

ABOUT THE AUTHOR

JB SCHROEDER, a graduate of Penn State University's creative writing program, writes both contemporary romance and romantic suspense—in other words: *romance to make your heart race*. She adores stories about everyday people embracing new beginnings—especially when the characters need a little help from true love.

www.jbschroederauthor.com

9 781943 561209